中英雙語

Letters to My Son

給愛兒的
二十封信

簡 宛 著
簡 宛・石 廷・Dr. Jane Vella 譯
杜曉西 繪

名作家簡宛筆下 20 則最細膩的親子對話，
陪青春期孩子看見自己，擁抱生命的無限可能。

國家圖書館出版品預行編目資料

給愛兒的二十封信－Letters to My Son / 簡宛著;簡宛,
石廷,Dr. Jane Vella譯;杜曉西繪.－－三版四刷.－－
臺北市: 三民,2018
　　面;　　公分.－－(愛閱雙語叢書)
中英對照
ISBN 978–957–14–5903–5　(平裝)

856.286　　　　　　　　　　　　　　　103007335

© 給愛兒的二十封信－Letters to My Son

著 作 人	簡　宛
譯　　者	簡　宛　　石　廷　　Dr. Jane Vella
繪　　者	杜曉西
發 行 人	劉振強
著作財產權人	三民書局股份有限公司
發 行 所	三民書局股份有限公司
	地址　臺北市復興北路386號
	電話　(02)25006600
	郵撥帳號　0009998–5
門 市 部	(復北店)臺北市復興北路386號
	(重南店)臺北市重慶南路一段61號
出版日期	初版一刷　2005年2月
	三版一刷　2014年5月
	三版四刷　2018年11月修正
編　　號	S805200

行政院新聞局登記證局版臺業字第○二○○號

ISBN　978-957-14-5903-5　（平裝）

http://www.sanmin.com.tw　三民網路書店
※本書如有缺頁、破損或裝訂錯誤,請寄回本公司更換。

改版序

　　《給愛兒的二十封信》，是國語日報邀請我為年輕學子所寫的作品，那時我與外子在臺北客座一年，對於臺灣的終身教育、家庭、婦女以及青少年教育都有比較深入的了解，而這本書中的文字，記錄了我對青少年的關懷。

　　這本書的完成，要感謝很多人的愛護與協助，外子是永遠支持者，長子石全的童年給我的靈感，次子石廷的英譯，我的老師簡維理教授的英文潤飾，三民書局董事長劉振強先生多年來的信賴和支持，外文組的編輯們認真負責的專業精神，都使我銘記在心。還有特別要感謝陸以正老師在百忙中的指正，更使我受益匪淺。

　　本書出版以來，廣受讀者的青睞，我們同時也陸續接到各方的建議與指教，主要意見是在於英譯部分文字運用較深，筆者考慮到希望此書能服務更廣大的讀者群，因此決定進行改版，將全書英譯部分重新潤飾，以利讀者能更輕鬆領略語言之美。

　　這次改版的方向，主要是針對英文譯文，希望能在保留中文精神的原則下，讓英文能夠更口語化、生活化；同時也把因為翻譯的關係，而未能完全表達的中文情緒，做再一次的補足並重新潤飾，讓英文譯文可以較為全面的表達原來的中文意境，可讀性更強。

　　經過將近一年的努力，「給愛兒的二十封信」終於完成增訂並即將出版，在此希望此增訂版，能讓讀者以更為輕鬆愉快的心情，享受學習和閱讀的樂趣。筆者能力有限，若有不當之處，尚祈讀者惠正。

Preface
to the Second Revised Edition

Letters to My Son came about when Mandarin Daily News invited me to write a series of articles for younger readers. At the time, I was accompanying my husband on a one-year sabbatical in Taiwan. Thus I had great interest in the issues and questions Taiwan's young adults were facing. This book records my thoughts during that time, and also reflects my care for Taiwan's next generation.

The completion of this book would not have been possible without the care and attention of many people, notably my husband Jason for his lifelong support; my elder son Giles, who inspired me during his childhood, my younger son Tim and my professor Dr. Jane Vella for help with translation and refining my English. I thank Mr. Liu Chen-Chiang, the president of San Min Book Company, for his constant trust and support; the editors for very professional and meticulous corrections. Also, a special thank-you to Mr. Lu Yi-Zheng for making time to offer his suggestions—I learned much from him and have greatly benefited from his input.

The Revised Second Edition aims at this book's English translation. We retained the essence of the Chinese original but only made the sentences more like spoken and everyday English. Taking this opportunity, we also modified some original English passages that couldn't fully reflect their Chinese counterparts due to the lack of equivalence, and made the English translation more corresponding to Chinese and more readable.

Through the nearly one-year effort, the revision of *Letters to My Son* is finally completed and is about to be published. I hope this revision could help the readers enjoy reading and learning in a more relaxing way. I also welcome all the valuable opinions regarding this book.

Jane Wan

給愛兒的二十封信　目次

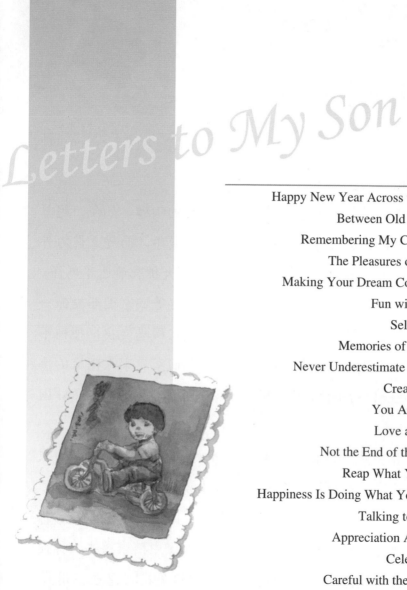

Letters to My Son

Index

■ 繞著地球賀新年

親愛的正兒：

我們回到臺北了。

回家鄉過年，是爸爸想了二十多年的心願，如今，總算如願以償，其快樂可想而知。甚至因為過年，而趕上從海外回國過年的人潮，機場入境處人山人海，大排長龍也不為怪。反正回家都是好的，就像在美國，人人趕著回家過耶誕節一樣，免不了飛機脫班、誤點，有人甚至在機場過夜，種種不便，也都能忍受，因為心中的意願──回家與家人團聚的快樂，蓋過一切的不快，人人都有一副好心情去接受眼前的「困境」。

這實在是一個很好的發現，用好心情去面對不好的狀況，竟然連「不好」的狀況，也會改觀，也不那麼討厭了。其實，這也是你和哥哥教會我的「本事」，每年耶誕節時，你們從外地趕回家過節，也都是在機場人潮中擠來擠去，你從小就不大情緒化，所以碰到這種事，你總是說：「急也沒用」，一路拿著速寫本，沿途畫著你愛的汽車和眾生百相，一副樂在其中的「酷」模樣。

可是，小時候，你這種「不在乎」的脾氣，可真急壞媽咪了，你天生是一個自由自在的孩子，從來不哭鬧，但也不會被牽著鼻子走。上學，不到時間不起床。做功課，自己有一套自動自發的計畫。現在你長大了，我常得意的對你說：「幸好媽媽給你一套有紀律的讀書習慣。」你也很幽默的說：「幸好，媽媽沒有用高壓逼迫我。」

好了，這次我和老爸也「酷」呆了，只差沒像你一樣拿速寫本一路畫圖。連「行李」掉了，也瀟灑的說：「沒關係，明天行李到了再送來好了。」兩人逍遙的步出機場，害小舅舅開了大車要來運行李，也無用武之地。

臺北年節的氣氛很濃，但是比起我們小時候，可差多了，沒有鞭炮，也沒有張燈結綵，不過比起在美國，可就有「氣氛」多了。在美國，感恩節或耶誕節才是大節日，家家戶戶喜氣洋洋。中國新年都是在上課期間，上班上課照常進行，因此你們上中小學時，媽媽總不忘到學校去教一些中國習俗、文化，請小朋友回家一起過年，所以也養成了你們過年的傳統習俗。當然，年年有「壓歲錢」是最難忘的習俗，連我到了臺北後，哥哥還打電話來，「爸爸媽媽，恭喜發財，紅包拿來。」

今年過年，我們一家四口，分住三家，記否我教過你的詩句：「一處鄉心五處同」？我們在美國時，自從你們上了大學後，也都是如此各分西東，好在爸媽知道你和哥哥都好好的在學習，也就安心了。

「父母在，不遠遊」是至聖先師孔夫子的名言，現在科技發達，世界越來越小，我們已經改成：「我們一起繞著地球跑」。只要我們好好學習，好好生活，電子郵件、傳真和電話，隨時可把我們連在一起。

我們在心裡互相祝福，在地球的不同角落向大家恭賀——新年快樂，身體健康，心想事成。

愛你的媽

■ 新舊之間

親愛的姪兒：

　　早晨起來，臺北在一片濛濛細雨中。過年期間的臺北反而安靜，沒有嘈雜的車，因為環保的關係，也沒有炮竹聲。我站在窗前，看著窗外的街景，忍不住想起你們，也想起我的童年。

　　小時候，差不多到了十二月，就每天期待著過年，首先，我們最感到興奮的是可以穿新衣買新鞋，在那個時代，一年只買一件新衣，不像現在天天有新衣穿，鞋子也是穿到通底了才換。阿媽很會做衣服，有時還把大人的舊衣服改了給我們穿，所以只有新年時候的新衣服，才是真正的新衣。因為我是老大，上了中學後，買新衣、新鞋，都是我帶著弟弟妹妹上臺北買，那真是一件好大好大的「大事」。

　　當年的中和鄉，還很偏僻，沒有公車，要到華江橋過河才有三輪車，可是我們也不怕麻煩，因為是「大事」，所以好早就安排，並且約了朋友，浩浩蕩蕩上臺北。

　　對於新衣服的喜悅，記憶還在，但是對於整個環境的窮和苦，已經忘記，現在想起來，反而有些「溫馨」和「甜蜜」。

為什麼？你一定會問，沒有電視，沒有玩具，沒有一切現代化的設備，怎麼還會「快樂」，太不可思議了。

你知道為什麼嗎？因為我們的生活中有安全感，有愛和關懷。這說起來很奇妙，可是千真萬確。而且我們常常用「想像」來做遊戲。

想像那一根竹子是馬，手推著馬，一搖一搖的跑起來，就是騎馬奔馳，配上戲詞，不正是歌仔戲上的一幕？想像那切下的柚子皮，白的部分是肥肉，粉紅的部分是瘦肉，用兩枝筷子當秤子，這樣就可玩起做生意的「家家酒」。或者在一張神明桌的下面，搭一塊小帳棚，就是很像樣的房子了，你小時候也玩過的遊戲，記得不？

在遊戲中，在沒有壓力下，童年的生活，海闊天空，餓了渴了，回家總有人，不是只有電視機和玩具的空房子。玩太瘋了，爸爸媽媽呵責兩句，很正常，有人關心有人疼，當時很不高興，現在想起來，很甜蜜。現在阿公阿媽都過世了，也沒人罵我了，心中卻很懷念他們。想念被愛的日子。

媽媽常常跟你們說，新衣服、新玩具是用錢買的，但不是最好最重要的東西，有些東西不必花錢去買，但是永遠值得保留。你小時候不太明白，中學時，喜歡穿名牌，我教了你一句「良馬不在毛」的成語，你也說了一句「良馬又有好毛更好」的頗富挑戰性的話，給我許多思考。「良馬又有好毛」固然很好，但次序上，良馬的內在，才是永久可貴，你終於明白了「真誠」與「自然」的風格，過了青少年後，名牌也不那麼吸引你了。畢竟你也長大了。

新舊之間有很大的空間，新衣、新鞋……在擁有的時候，真的很快樂，但是，能夠流傳下來，成了古董，成了回憶的一部分，更能令人回味無窮。

新年裡，懷念的都是陳年往事，因為那是長存我心底的可貴珍藏，不知你在新年中可有什麼值得回憶的事？

愛你的媽

■ 童年往事

親愛的远兒：

　　早晨起來，看到太陽露出了笑臉，好高興，趕快穿上球鞋，出門慢跑。

　　因為行李未到，我們先住在舅舅家，也就是媽媽小時候住過的地方，我慢慢走到附近中和國小，忍不住進去看看，我和阿姨及舅舅，都是中和國小畢業的，對於最早上學的地方，一直非常懷念。學校已經改變許多，操場變小了，樓房加多了，十二月的風輕輕的吹過樹梢，我站在操場的中央，想著兒時在這兒玩躲避球、拔河比賽，還有學騎腳踏車……許許多多童年的回憶，全跑到眼前。

　　小學的時候，社會普遍樸實，生活也非常簡單，尤其在鄉下，許多孩子都打光腳上學，我好羨慕，因為一到中午休息時間，他們就到河裡嬉水摸魚。有一次我也忍不住偷偷把鞋子和襪子脫了，下去和他們玩，卻不小心跌倒了，全身溼透，腳底還被玻璃刮破流血，非常的狼狽，回到家，還被阿公罰站了一下午，這個慘痛的經驗，至今印象深刻。我那時小小心靈一直感到愧咎，因為是我不乖、不聽話，所以上天在責罰我才會跌跤。這個自責，也使我不敢再「背著爸爸媽

媽」赤足下水了。

　　我們那個時候一班有五十多人，年紀從八歲到十二歲都
有。因為老師管教很嚴，上課不准外出，也不能走動，一年
級的時候，常常有人「尿褲子」，有人升到二三年級了，還是
有這個現象。我後來學了教育心理學，提出這個問題在班上
討論，一致的看法就是年幼的孩子，自制力不夠，環境改變
或心理緊張，都會尿溼褲子。不知現在的小學生，上課時間
是不是已經可以自由出入教室了？你們在小學的時候，一班
只有二十幾人，有兩個老師教你們，我有時去當義工，常常
被全班活潑亂動的孩子，弄得筋疲力盡。比起美國的孩子，
臺灣的小孩真是安靜又老成。我常常在想，東西合璧，兩者
之間稍稍平衡一下多好！

　　我慢慢走出校園，陽光開始照耀大地，孩子們陸陸續續
背著書包走入校門，他們都好有禮貌
的對著我微笑，路上還有小警察在維
持交通，我感到一股朝氣。在故鄉的
土地上，看著那如朝陽般可愛的
笑臉，感覺生命的傳承和活力，
心中充滿希望的愉悅。

愛你的媽

■ 爬山的快樂

親愛的泓兒：

　　我們已搬入了新居。

　　新居在南港，臺北的東北面，附近有山，天氣好的時候，可以登高望遠，將臺北盆地收在眼底，非常壯麗。在美國東部北卡羅萊納州住久了，好像爬山的機會很少，因為美國的地形，東部大都為老年期的山，中部是大平原，西部落磯山系才有許多雄偉的山脈。所以對於我生長的故鄉，尤其是我童年、青少年時常爬的山，也就特別的懷念。

　　因為臺灣處處有山可登，有名勝可探，每次回來，我都不放過可以爬山的機會。住在臺北近郊，處處是起早登山的健行者，一大早扶老攜幼，呼吸新鮮的空氣，有時還聽得到鳥叫。南港附近，有短程三十分鐘可走完的山，也有兩三小時可以翻越的山，從這個山進到另一個山口，再坐公車回來。二姨已經迫不及待的要和媽媽去登高探勝了。

　　媽媽最抱歉的是，你們小時候沒有常常帶你們去爬山，因為我們住家附近都是平地，最靠近我們的名山，大煙山系，也要開五小時的車才到。你和哥哥小的時候，我們還常去露營，到蒙思山、皮士卡山玩，但是，媽媽對露營興趣不大，有時爸爸帶了你和哥哥參加四健會 (4-H) 去滑雪，媽媽不愛去，怕摔斷骨頭，害得你們也少了這方面的活動。

　　為什麼媽媽不愛露營呢？這是有原因的，我們剛到美國不久的一個夏天，那時你還沒出生呢！哥哥才兩歲多，我們去紐約州北部的千島 (Thousand Islands) 露營，大伙兒一起好高興，搭起帳棚，唱歌、烤肉，可是，半夜卻下起雨來了，越下越大，幾小時都沒停過。那時的露營地區設備不如今日齊全，氣溫又因雨而下降，我和爸爸深怕哥哥受涼，只好把哥哥抱在車上，把暖氣打開，又怕車子發動太久，把電用盡，所以緊張萬分。哥哥一路都睡得很好，不吵不鬧，但是可把爸爸和我累慘了。從此一談起露營，我們一定不會忘記這件往事的教訓，總是多準備毛毯和防雨設備，但是太費周章，一向愛化繁為簡，不喜歡麻煩的我，也就捨繁就簡，選擇海濱為我們全家度假的地點了。

不過在臺灣可不同了，臺灣有三分之二的地形是山系，我們小時候遠足就常常去爬山，上了大學以後的活動，也以登山郊遊為主要的休閒活動。下次你來臺北玩，我一定帶你去爬爬臺北近郊的山。「高瞻遠矚」，是一個很好的人生境界，「登泰山而小天下」，正是如此。也只有常常登高遠眺，用廣角看世界，才會避免孤芳自賞，做井底蛙的自限，希望你也能養成這種習慣，也拓展視野。

　　好了，我要去爬山健行了，就此擱筆，下次再談。

愛你的媽

■ 你可使夢想成真

親愛的正兒：

你好嗎？

昨天和爸爸去參觀一個健康俱樂部，爸爸愛游泳，一到室內游泳池就愛上了，立即入會，成了會員，今天迫不及待的去游泳了。

對於游泳，我是門外漢，比較喜歡做韻律操，跳有氧舞蹈，對於許多球類、田徑等，都很低能。這很可能是小時候種下的「排斥」心理。

我小時候，因為不小心掉到水裡，對水一向懷著恐懼的心理。那時候會游泳的人也不多，老是聽到誰誰在河裡洗澡，踩到深水處，淹死了。又聽到一些孩子在河中玩，被「水鬼」牽走的傳說。種種恐怖的傳說與事實，使我對「水」敬而遠之，到了二十歲，都還沒下水的經驗。

這種「害怕」的心理，我現在懂了心理學之後，當然明白是很容易去解除的。尤其在你們小的時候，媽媽更不想用自己心裡所怕的事物去影響你們，所以只好先自己克服，去面對「害怕」的事。你們很小就學會游泳了，我也很「勇敢」

的與你們一起去 YMCA 學，可是「老狗學新技」，可真不容易呢！你們一下子就學會了，我卻只停留在「浮」、「沈」的階段，對水的恐懼是消除了，但是，泳技，也只夠用在欣賞別人的時候。對於你們的水中表現，我都是給予最熱烈的掌聲，在我心中，你們實在是「好棒」、「好能幹」的游泳健將呢！

現在面對著一池溫水，多麼想跳下去做一條快樂的魚兒，但是，游一下要站起來換氣，再怎麼快樂，也還是不能有「暢遊」的快樂。

「自己把自己困住」正是如此，恐懼心，加上自卑感，加上「決心不夠」，都是阻礙自己往前走的「絆腳石」，許多兒時的陰影，如果不解除，到大了就越來越難了。這使我想起在美國時，有朋友參加「飛行俱樂部」，因為對空中旅行有恐懼症，所以每次坐飛機都如臨大敵，相信這種人不少，受過訓之後，面對飛行的事實，了解狀況之後，就再也不害怕了。

　　所以我要告訴你的是，以後對什麼事沒信心，或害怕時，就設法找出害怕的真相，並加以了解，這樣就可以因了解而增加信心。好比在黑暗中，摸索著找路，如果先有概念，找到地圖，辨別了方向，再黑的路也不害怕了。對不對？

　　下次有什麼害怕的事，就設法去了解它，面對它，那麼就沒有什麼事會阻礙你了，這樣，許許多多的夢想都有實現的可能了。

愛你的媽

■ 書中歲月

親愛的巧兒：

今天好快樂。

下了好多天的雨，今天雨終於停了，我趕快出門，走到中央研究院。雖然外面車聲隆隆，院內倒是很安靜，我參觀了許多館，最後走到圖書館，更叫我歡喜，不僅有許多資料、期刊，還有研究報告。我一向愛看書，這一年，不是等於入了寶山了嗎？有這麼多書可以好好享受。

說到看書，上圖書館，就想起你小時候陪媽媽讀書的往事。那時你才兩歲多吧？媽媽在伊利諾大學研究所修兒童文學，每週要讀近百本的兒童書，我就帶了你上圖書館，你和媽媽一樣，也背了小包包，不過裡面不是筆記本，而是蠟筆和紙。我們坐在圖書館的小椅子，你看書看煩了，就把蠟筆和紙拿出來畫圖，有時候坐不住了，又站起來去飲水機喝水。圖書館的人，看你那麼小，又那麼可愛，就不斷的誇獎你，你一被誇，更要表現得乖，有小孩大聲說話，你會把小手指放在唇上。

「噓！」

　　我至今還記得你那可愛的模樣呢！

　　我相信讀書的習慣都是從小養成的，你陪媽咪上圖書館，也跟著煞有其事的看圖畫書，那時，你最愛看里奧尼的故事書，因為色彩很鮮豔。記得那本《小黃和小藍》嗎？我至少說了十次，你甚至會背了，還是愛這本書。結果有一天，媽媽的好朋友藍阿姨和黃阿姨來家裡玩，你盯著她們兩人看，堅持要她們兩人抱在一起，我們都不懂你為什麼這麼奇怪，但也笑著依了你，等到她們兩人坐下來時，你才奇怪的問：

　　「可是藍阿姨和黃阿姨為什麼沒有變成綠阿姨呢？」說得我們大笑不已，差點從椅子上滾下來。

　　原來《小黃和小藍》的書中，兩人相碰之後，就變成了綠色。我想，你對顏色的認識，也是從那時候開始的，很小就喜歡畫圖，並且加上各種顏色。

　　啊！都是好多年前的事了，媽媽大概是很想念你，忍不住一直提你幼年的事。你一個人在美國，過年還好嗎？功課那麼忙，大概也沒心去中國城吃一頓，等你回臺灣時，再好好補請你好了。

愛你的媽

■ 自尊

親愛的姪兒：

你的信收到了。

你問起什麼是「自尊」？是否就是英文中的 "Self-esteem"？你對中英雙語的比較如此有興趣，真好。記不記得那年你來臺北國語日報中心學國語的情形？那時你還很不情願呢！若不是在學習中碰到了好朋友，又有好老師耐心教導你，你大概就變成真正的「香蕉」了。（註：香蕉即指外黃內白，外表黃種人，可是一句中文也不會，像洋人的華人。）

自尊，不錯，就是與英文中 Self-esteem 相似。每個人都需要有自尊，但是自尊不是自傲。在青少年時，每個孩子的情緒起起落落，一下子高興，一下子又不理人，你記得你自己這個年紀時的特點嗎？

有自尊心的人，特點是：可以自動自發去做事，有榮譽感，有責任心，面對困難時，也不會退縮。

沒有自尊的人，比較容易消極、怨天尤人，事情做不好時，往往半途而廢，最明顯的現象是，沒有主見，容易被人左右、牽著鼻子走。

　　譬如說學習語文，在海外的華人下一代，就是你們，沒有一個人認為學習華文是容易的，但是有人半途放棄，有人堅持下去。放棄的人，總是說：太難了，學中文有什麼用？堅持下去的人，總是認為，我不信我學不會，別人做得到，我想也不應該太難吧！

　　一念之間，難易之別。

　　可是在小小年紀的時候，沒有一個小孩會自己知道要「由心轉念」這種事，你們的自尊心，與爸媽及老師的態度有密切的關係，如果父母老是說你「笨死了」、「你怎麼老學不好」，老師又每天批評你，挑剔你沒有別人學得好，在小小心靈中，受到的「挫折感」就很深，久而久之，就失去自信，也就沒有自尊心了，因為連自己也相信自己不如別人了嘛！「我好笨」，一句話，就把自己判了刑，多可惜！

你運氣好，碰到了好老師，一路學習過來，都是肯定與鼓勵，自然，長大了，也就不大麻煩爸爸媽媽了。我常常跟朋友說，不要老指責孩子；我也跟小朋友說，不要氣餒、自卑，你不愛自己，誰愛你呢？爸媽很愛你們，但有時也會「不小心」傷了你們的自尊，使你們烙下自卑的印痕。你和哥哥最常說的是：「我是我嘛!」

　　好了不起，我是我嘛!

　　因為你是你，獨一無二的你，所以你要有自己值得人尊重的風格。

　　人必自尊而後人尊之，這是要從小養成的習慣。

　　我們尊重你。也希望你能養成自尊之人的習慣。

愛你的媽

■ 閣樓上的回憶

親愛的宝兒：

　　媽媽常常跟你提起的老家——我出
生的地方，那個房子，比我的年紀還大，
我一直住到結婚時才離開，所以你也可以
想像我與老家的感情有多深！

　　老家的屋宇很高，全是鋼筋水泥建成
的，在當年，是非常時髦的房子，外面還全是白色的磁磚，
如今已老舊，我還記得小時候有地震，許多鄰居都跑到我們
家躲避，因為房子牢固不會被地震壓垮。

　　我們兒時最愛去也最感神秘的地方，就是老家的閣樓，
我們玩捉迷藏遊戲時，躲到閣樓上最安全，因為閣樓很高且
暗，只有從天窗射入的陽光，灑在閣樓的地板上，構成很詩
意的光圈。我初中時，讀《小婦人》，讀到老二「喬」每日在
閣樓上，關起門來偷偷寫作，我也幻想我自己躲在閣樓上編
白日夢的快樂。那個時候，弟弟妹妹全擠在一起，共用房間，

我是多麼希望閣樓上有一個角落，是屬於我自己的天地。可是，因為閣樓上沒燈，我也只好熄滅了那「偷偷躲在閣樓上」編夢的渴望。

多少年的歲月流逝，現在站在閣樓上，藉著天窗流入的陽光，許許多多的童年回憶全來到眼前，牆壁上有「石磨」，有「糕模」，石磨是用來磨糯米，壓乾後再做「糕」的。我們最愛幫忙做紅龜糕，有點像你們小時候在玩 Play Dough。還有斗笠和棕簑衣，是下雨天的雨具，已經成了古董。你大概從來都沒見過。下次要特別帶你見識一下。

最讓我感動的是一箱箱的書和筆記本，整整齊齊的放在櫃中或箱裡，都是阿媽親手整理的，上面有阿媽用手寫的註明，七個孩子，分門別類，連相本、紀念冊都還保留著，我一邊翻著，一邊忍不住淚水涔涔而下，我好想念我的母親。

記得臨回臺灣的前一個月，正好是耶誕節，我們也在一起整理東西。你童年的文具、獎狀、第一張圖畫，連第一個掉下來的小乳牙和小玩具熊都留下來，你大笑，「媽媽好山東饅頭 (Sentimental) 哦!」天下的父母都是一樣的，把孩子當心肝寶貝的疼著。你們大概要到做了父母，才能真正領會這種心意。只有一件事我確實的感覺到，在愛中長大的孩子，童年的回憶充滿鼓舞的力量。我倒不太在意你會不會像我一樣珍惜這些陳年的寶貝，但是，我希望我們能給予你們的是人生中鼓舞的力量，當你長大，當你也做了父母，回憶童年往事，也使你感受到綿綿相傳的愛心和親情，也用同樣包容的愛對待每一個人。

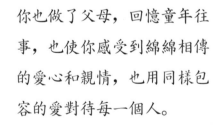

　　閣樓上的陽光，仍然灑滿在地板上，歲月流轉，經過了多少寒暑堆積著越來越多的回憶和懷念。像那越積越多的愛，在我心中綻放。

　　媽媽想念你。

愛你的媽

■ 不要低估自己

親愛的兒兒：

　　今天一早出門，和上學的孩子們擠公車，現在的公共汽車和以前我們做學生的時候不一樣了，班次多，路線也多，其實也不算太擠，比起我們以前像「沙丁魚罐頭」一樣，擠得水洩不通，那真是不可同日而言。

　　我的座位旁邊，有幾個中學生在談話，我問他們幾年級，他們說：「國三。」那就是等於美國的「八年級生」！他們不斷的擔憂著快要來臨的考試，一再的說著自己多麼差勁，完全沒有信心，對前途沒有希望。

　　我忍不住想起十幾歲時的孩子，是不是都背負著這麼大的負擔？我不記得你在這個年紀的時候，有他們那麼重的包袱，想得那麼多？你那時參加足球隊，又學鋼琴和繪畫，還和同學組織了舞蹈團體，贏得了才藝表演首獎，每天也是過得很忙碌，但是我倒記得你那個年紀時，和他們一樣有對自己不太能確定的「迷惑」。

　　你也許不夠壯，又不夠帥，牙齒又不整齊（正綁著整牙器），和別的孩子站在一起，又沒有捲髮高鼻，也不會要寶逗

笑⋯⋯但是，你是你呀！記不記得媽媽給你的「打氣」？

「你是你啊！」是媽媽先給你的定心丸。

你是你，你雖然長得和美國小孩不一樣，但是你有雙重文化的背景，你會中英文語言，你有你的才能，看，你會畫畫，又會打球，又會自編自導跳「雷步」(Rap Dance)，前途等你去「開發」，多麼令人羨慕啊！我今天也是用同樣的話和年輕的中學生說：「你只有一個你，即使全世界都不稱讚你、鼓勵你，你自己可不能放棄給自己鼓掌、讚美的機會，沒有什麼好擔心的。」

是不是很有效？用肯定的態度對自己，你還有許許多多愛你、關心你的人，像老師、爸爸媽媽、

哥哥、阿姨、舅舅、姑姑⋯⋯哇，想起來沒？數一數就明白，自己實在不應該把自己「否定」，因為全世界只有一個你，「獨一無二」的你啊！

不過十幾歲時，不會去想這麼多美好的事。也許那個年齡正是「少年不知愁滋味，為賦新詩強說愁」，少不了有「少年維特的煩惱」那種趨勢。記住，不要去想自己沒有的、不如人的地方，多想想自己「與眾不同」之處，你自認自己「最得意之處」，像你的舞姿，你的球藝，你的聲音⋯⋯把自己的特點顯露出來，那就是「酷」，絕不是用錢可以買來的「流行」。

考壞了，沒關係，還有下一次，你盡了心力就好。但是，你若是用否定把自己打倒，永遠悲觀、消極，你就損失太大了，不要低估了自己。

你覺得媽咪的話有理嗎？

愛你的媽上

不要低估自己

■ 愛作怪的你

親愛的巨兒：

　　外面正下著傾盆大雨，臺北的雨季，聽說就要開始了。我站在窗前，對著雨中的街景發呆，許多事，因為下雨而令人卻步，本來想去看畫展的心情，頓時意興索然。突然，我看到一個小孩，拉著他的媽媽，打著傘，在雨中走來走去，一點也不在乎雨水的侵襲，好像口中還哼著歌呢！那景象，多麼像兒時的你？

　　你小時候也是喜歡在雨中玩水，或在雪地上打滾。有一天，本來計畫好要出門野餐，因為下雨了，我就懶得出門，你好失望，一個人伏在窗口，念念有詞的唱著：「雨啊雨啊！我好想出去玩水，可是我的媽媽怕你，她也不讓我出去，你快快停了好不好？」看著你那可愛的樣子，我只好打了傘牽著你的小手，在雨中的路上賞雨。也許是這份不受環境左右的童心，也因此開啟了我已經「老化」或已經「封閉」的心靈，產生了許多童心與童趣，也創造了生活中的情趣。

從你的身上，我拾回了赤子之心。我常常覺得成人有太多的「顧慮」和「限制」，因此也產生了消極與退縮的負面影響，我真希望你能永遠保持這份開朗、樂觀的天性。可是年歲越長，你好像也越多「困惑」，尤其在青少年的時期，你幾乎是對自己完全否定，沒有信心，又不知如何處理情緒，幸好是你天性中那種自由自在的特點，使你平衡下來。你用創作，用繪畫，用舞蹈，用與眾不同的裝扮，「秀」出你的內心世界，你也教會了爸爸和媽媽，如何用另一個角度去欣賞你，而不是批判你，去包容你的不按牌理出牌，而不是用傳統的框框限制你。

記不記得你腦後一絡「老鼠尾巴」？從十歲留到十二歲，多麼的標新立異？可是當人人都流行這種髮型時，你卻毅然剪掉。你也會把爸爸的襯衫袖子剪掉，設計成「垮垮」的樣子，還入選學校最流行的服裝。在 L.A. BOYZ 還沒出道前，你與幾個死黨設計舞步，幾乎把我們家地板跳垮了，電視邀約不斷，多少人想要的才藝表演，可是，你們瘋過之後，各自拿了申請到的獎學金，說：「我們上大學了，以學業為重，不再表演。」而拒絕了電視臺的邀請。

　　爸媽冷眼旁觀，愛呆了你這份「酷」勁。你儘管作怪、瘋狂，也有情緒的起起落落，但是，始終沒有忘了你的「責任」——好好讀書。「大學四年全額獎學金，也不是隨便可以得到的。」你常常很自我負責的對我說，「媽媽，你可以信任我。」

　　我真的是很信任你，因為我知道你是一個與眾不同的孩子，從那一天，你在雨中踩水、跳躍，我就知道，我們不能用框框，用教條限制你。

　　我希望全天下的母親，與她們的孩子，都能一起走回童年，製造共同回憶。

　　　　　　　　　　　　　愛你的媽

■ 你很好，你不差勁！

親愛的远兒：

　　今天在公車上，碰到許多放學的小朋友，每人臉上都好疲倦的樣子。我主動找他們談天，起先，大家都不大好意思說話，後來，比較自在了，突然有一個小朋友說：「我們好忙好累呵！不知道怎麼去應付這麼多的功課？覺得自己好差勁！」

　　我看到他們青春的臉上，有許多焦慮和迷惑，這個年紀，不是應該快快樂樂的過日子嗎？怎麼已經嚴肅得笑不出來了？記得你在這個年紀時，也是忙得不知如何安排時間，可是，你不是為考試，是為了功課以外的活動，打球，社交，欣賞音樂，參加派對等等；在時間的安排和運用上，缺少組織與規劃的能力，尤其是，如果還想在課後又學一些才藝，或打工賺錢，那不是更窮於應付了嗎？

　　忙碌，時間不夠用，幾乎是現代人的通病，想不到年輕的孩子，也有了這早到的壓力，這同時也表示，年少的孩子，正開始告別童稚、面對自己和責任，要學習處理時間，管理自己的生活了。我也想告訴你，其實，感到時間的不夠分配，進而學習處理壓力，也是你成長中很重要的課題呢！

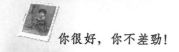

處理壓力最好的辦法就是學會說「不」，拒絕一些活動，如果樣樣事都要參加，又要參加活動，又要玩樂，又有功課，當然會感到吃不消。所以最好的辦法就是選一兩樣自己喜歡的活動，輪流做，不必一下子要一把捉，全部都參加，或什麼玩樂都要享受，電視、電影，一樣不肯缺，自然應接不暇。

青春的歲月，是讓你學習欣賞生活中的點點滴滴，學校的功課，增加你的學識；朋友的感情，讓你感到友情的珍貴；課外活動，使你學會人際禮儀及鍛鍊自己的身心平衡；即使是學琴、學畫，也是培養自己的嗜好和專長。但是，記住，不必樣樣逞能逞強，凡事要爭第一，最重要的是學習的「過程」。你在打球練琴之中，得到快樂更甚於拿了錦標歸，因為太求好求勝的心理，有時會把自己的興趣和信心完全忽略，甚至扼殺，那就完全失去學習的意義了。

我跟那個小朋友說：「你很好，你一點也不差勁。」

重要的是學會自己做時間的主人，而不是讓時間追著你，給你壓力和焦慮。學著拒絕，也學會面對拒絕，生活中，有自己的選擇，也就有了許多空間，這也是我長大後才學會的事，特與你分享。

愛你的媽

■ 愛與真誠

親愛的丹兒：

　　上星期有一位名叫光建的學生來找我，他滿臉焦慮，像很多在學的學生一樣，擔心功課、交友、家庭以及未來前途等等。昨天他又來找我，看起來比上次更愁眉不展。

　　我問他：「怎麼了，光建？」

　　「我爸爸和媽媽又吵架了，他們總是吵個不休，我沒辦法做功課。我媽媽叫我爸爸搬出去。」

　　「真是不妙！」我安慰光建：「告訴我，我能幫你做什麼事？」

　　光建說：「謝謝。我沒辦法跟我父母討論這件事，因為他們總是吵吵鬧鬧，要不就是罵我。我在學校也沒交到什麼好朋友，我真不知該怎麼辦？」

　　我可以想像光建的挫折感，他使我想起你小學四年級時，有一天放學回家，顯露出從沒有過的悶聲不響，你說是因為你的好朋友艾瑞克的事，但不肯告訴我們發生了什麼事。

　　好幾天之後，你還是愁眉不展，最後終於忍不住問我：「媽媽，你和爸爸會離婚嗎？我們家會分開嗎？」

　　「你在說什麼啊？」我嚇一跳，「為什麼問這個問題？」

「因為艾瑞克的爸爸媽媽要離婚了，他們一家分成兩半……」淚流滿面的你，露出了你幼小心靈的疑慮。

我趕忙把你摟在懷裡，擦乾你的淚水，並且肯定的對你說：「不用擔心，爸爸和媽媽不會離婚，我們家會永遠在一起。」對稚齡的你，那是你最需要的定心丸，你聽後立即破涕為笑，像陽光從雲層中露出了光華。

聽到你一些朋友家庭間，父母離婚和分居的故事，也許年幼的你們以為很多家庭都會分開，那對家庭中相親相愛的信心就跟著消失。當然，如果這個負面的想法或疑惑一直存在著，那就會不斷地腐蝕心中的信念。

我們永不讓這種負面的想法或疑慮發生在我們家。

你記不記得我翻譯的那本《愛、生活與學習》的書？它提醒著大家，若為人父母不曾對孩子表達愛心，或父母彼此間不相愛，孩子長大成人後，也會對愛失去信心。愛，必須從愛中學習，也唯有從愛的行動中才能得到愛。有了愛才會有信念——那是對家庭，對我們自己以及對生命的真信念。

希望我們給了你一個好的榜樣，你也有所領悟，並且永遠記住真愛無懼，從真愛中才能產生真誠。

祝福你有快樂的一天。

愛你的媽

■ 不是世界末日

親愛的兒兒：

　　今天早上，天灰濛濛的，我的心情也跟著低落，尤其看到報上一個十二歲的小女孩自殺了，我的眼睛一邊讀著報，一邊就下起了雨。

　　啊！我也想起了你的同學強尼，那一個一頭金髮的可愛小男生，常常坐我的車，我載你們去足球場踢球。他在一個春日的清晨，飛下四十號公路的陸橋，結束了才十三年的生命。

　　那個時候，為了怕悲傷的你，以及同學們心中的困惑與難過無法宣洩，我常常去學校參加你們的心理輔導，聽你們傾訴，與你們分擔心中的感覺，使我因此更加了解你們，並且對學校在處理這件事的態度，印象深刻。

　　學校完全採取「傾聽」的態度，聽你們敘述對逝者的懷念、感傷、震驚……沒有半點批判、

說教，讓你們充分的發洩心中想表達的情感，甚至語無倫次的話，也受到尊重。一到大家心中平穩了，又邀請校外的心理學家，來與大家談有關死亡與自殺的種種看法。

「嗯——想想看，這是你，天下獨一無二的你，你不愛惜自己，老跟自己過不去，別人會不會也如此對待你？」我記得曾經對你們談過內心的話，我還說：「青春，多麼好的年齡，你們的機會那麼好，樣樣事都可參與，不要放棄你成為贏家的機會。強尼，他選擇了短暫的生命，我們懷念他，但自殺，是消極否定的思想，會使你悲觀、退縮。其實，每個人只要想一想，生活中處處都是值得慶祝的事，自己也有許多值得自傲的優點，這一切都值得額手稱慶。」

記得那首歌嗎？我當年教你和哥哥唱的——

　　　　「太陽下山，明朝依舊爬上來，花兒謝了，明年還是一樣的開……」

　　　　睡個覺，明天又是新的一天，天大的事都不是「世界末日」。從那時起，「又不是世界末日」變成我們家的口頭禪，你們也學著用樂觀的笑容，迎接另一天的朝陽。雖然強尼的自殺使大家消沈，但陰霾已逐漸散去了。

人生的每一個階段，都是學習。在你的童稚年齡裡，除了友情，你也學習了生命中的生與死。

　　我也想在此，祝福所有的青春兒女。成長，本身就是一件美好的事，偶爾的失意、孤單、不如意，都會過去，生命就是如此展現著不同的面貌，我們活著，也學習著，這就是真實的人生。再也不要用「世界末日」來壓迫自己，因為每一天，都是一個新的開始。

　　　　　　　　　　　　　　　　　愛你的媽

不是世界末日

■ 種瓜得瓜

親愛的姪兒：

　　今天有朋友從外地來，我帶他們去參觀了研究院內的胡適紀念館。其實，在建築上，紀念館只是一間小屋子而已，並不特別引人。但是我想介紹的是藏在建築下豐沛的人文精神。在我的求學時代，胡適先生的那句話：「要怎麼收穫先那麼栽。」深刻的印在我心上，對我影響至深。我一直相信天下沒有不勞而獲的成果。也許，這正是我帶朋友參觀紀念館的用心。

　　記得你小時候，學校常常有「動手做」的活動，現在的臺北很流行，稱之為 "DIY" (Do It Yourself)。我們都很喜歡這種活動，有時是一小粒種籽，有時是一小棵花苗，有時是一塊木板，或是一大堆彩色紙。花苗、種籽，埋在土中，要澆水施肥。木板、彩色紙要製成什麼玩具，得自己設計，我們都很用心的投入這種遊戲，也許不該叫遊戲，但那種學習過程好玩有趣，比遊戲還迷人。

人生，真的就是 DIY (Do It Yourself)——自己耕耘，沒有僥倖，因為是自己用心用手去做，整個過程也就充滿了快樂。

　　胡適之先生當年提倡白話文，必定經歷了許多阻力，但是他說出了「種瓜得瓜，種豆得豆」的經驗之談，正是至理名言。

　　對於學設計的你，這種經驗比什麼都真確。沒有感覺，必定也產生不了認知，沒有認知，當然就不會有去「做」的動力，用在日常生活中，真的是事事如此。想想看，如果你的決定是掌握在別人手中，如何會有衝勁去完成？當初如果我們用自己的意願強迫你去讀沒有興趣的科系，你如何會夜以繼日努力用功？

　　「一分耕耘一分收穫」其實是很淺顯的道理，不過常常在生活中被忽略了。

　　朋友參觀完紀念館，突然對我說：「我明白我孩子為什麼不用功了，因為所有的決定都是我替他做的，包括做功課與交朋友。這是我今天的收穫。」

　　我不知道這算不算也是我今天的收穫？

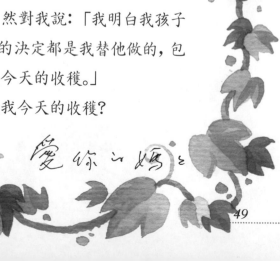

愛你的媽

■ 樂在用功

親愛的巨兒：

　　今天有三個中學生來與我談天，他們都是才上高中的學生，因為老師指定要訪問一位作者，寫讀書報告，所以他們就選定了與我談寫作經驗以及如何開拓自己的生涯規劃。

　　這使我想起許多事的源起，其實也是很偶然的。小時候，也許正巧寫對了一篇文章，或演講比賽得了獎，或與人辯論（小時候好辯）時占了上風，受到了鼓勵與讚美，於是信心大增，做起來也就不畏懼。這一切的出發點，也在於自己的興趣。受到了鼓勵而有興趣的事，這麼多年做下來，樂此不疲，越做（越寫）越有興趣。相反的，若受到排斥或挑剔，受到嘲弄或譏笑，也許從此就不會再有任何創作或發展的機會。

　　中小學的老師，對我的啟發非常大，我相信每個孩子在幼小時，都有許許多多的夢想，有些實現，有些幻滅，就是與受到老師正當的輔導有關。記不記得你小時候，用十字繡歪歪斜斜的繡了幾

個字，當做母親節的禮物——「媽咪我愛你」，送給我。老師因為班上只有你一個小男生拿針繡字，「受寵若驚」，大大的張揚，嚇得你再也不選這個課外活動，八歲以後，就不碰針線了。所以有時師長適當的態度與觀念，對於幼小孩子的啟發，意義重大。幸好，你把動手創作的興趣，轉移到汽車設計。

至於生涯規劃，我並不覺得我在小小年紀就明白。年紀小，心智未成熟，怎能替將來長大後，那一個更有智慧的自己，規劃出人生的藍圖？我們頂多也只是朝自己能做得好，有把握、有興趣的事，多下功夫，多努力。世界那麼寬廣，何必小小年紀就立下「做大事」的宏願？那壓力不是太大了嗎？

神話學家坎伯 (J. Campbell) 說過：「英雄旅程的目標，乃是你自己，找到你自己。」我記得一再對你和哥哥說過的話，也是要你們自己找到自己的興趣和專長。若以為是替爸爸媽媽讀書，或為一爭長短而努力，總歸是別人眼中的你，如果不快樂，或怨恨，「成大功，做大事」又怎麼樣？這是你們要明白並且對自己負責任的。

愛你的媽

■ 與自己對話

親愛的運兒：

這些日子來，忙著為各學校的家長成長班做講演，因此跟你的通信和電子郵件也拖延了。不過，我覺得自己在這些活動中，也學到了許多，我不用演講的方式，而用雙向溝通。大家好像輕輕鬆鬆的，卻在交流中，分享了親子教育的理念和方法。你一定記得，你們在青少年的時候，我也為你們學校做過的活動吧！

那個時候的你們，正是十幾歲的青少年時代，每個人外表都是雄糾糾氣昂昂的神氣活現，可是，心中好像也充滿了焦慮和恐慌，那也是正常的現象，因為你們身心都在變化，生理上，荷爾蒙的變化，使身體心理都處在敏感而容易衝動的狀況，情緒尤其不穩，

所以倒楣的就是爸爸媽媽或親近的家人或朋友了。因為情緒不穩，常常就有衝口而出，不經思索的言語，事後自己又後悔又難過，卻不知如何是好？

我做了一個「與自己對話」的演練，給你們自己去內省，因為從許多青少年的訪問中，我聽到了他們的心聲 ──「當我對爸媽大吼的時候，我心裡憎恨我自己。」

「當我對弟弟妹妹嫌煩時，我心裡不舒服。」

「當我應該拒絕時，卻口是心非的接受，我鄙視自己。」

「當我應該守信用時，卻不能履行諾言，我內疚。」

「當我應該幫助別人時，卻自私的視若無睹，我後悔。」

這些內心的不安和歉咎，有時會在心上留下太深的痕跡。如果沒有宣洩疏導，難免造成行為偏差。所以我常常在活動中，要求孩子們也寫下自己感覺很好的事項，譬如 ──「完成責任」、「用心盡力做完一件事之後的感覺」、「誠實的對待別人」、「幫助別人」等等。

隨時記錄並觀察自己的「感覺」，比較不會情緒化，也就是在情緒的智商──EQ 上，會產生自控能力。因此，我建議大家用一張紙，隨時寫下使自己自豪或自卑的事，例如：當我幫助老人或盲人過街時，我很快樂。

當我對爸媽或師長不禮貌時，我很後悔。……

我始終相信，誠實的面對自己，才是快樂的根本。

學習是使自己快樂的主要因素。每一個母親都希望自己的孩子，正常、健康、快樂。從她們的臉上，我彷彿看到了你們當年學習的神情。我時常在想，每一個心都是柔軟的，每一個孩子，都有一顆純淨向善的心，作為父母的我們，也是時時在用心學習，所以親子感情能在相親相愛中滋長。如果彼此能放下一些自我主張、自以為是的主觀，就非常圓滿。

你以為對嗎？

愛你的媽

■ 接受感謝

親愛的芷兒：

　　從 E-Mail 電子郵件中，知道你已回到學校，又開始忙於新的學年。很高興在假期中，你能回到臺北來小住，也重遊你五年不見的故鄉，尤其是與我同去臺中，與中興大學文學院的學生演講，這大概是第一次你坐在臺下，在中距離的「欣賞」你的媽媽吧！

　　在孩子的心目中，媽媽的形象是什麼呢？我突然很好奇的想知道。你在信上回答著我──

　　「長大後，我第一次這樣看待我的父母，」你信上寫著，「像一個第三者一樣，聽我媽媽談寫作，談生活，以及談我蹣跚學步的童年，那實在是一個美好的感覺。小時候我聽媽媽念故事，與爸爸媽媽一起釣魚，我一直在跟他們學習，可是我又不覺得是在學習，這一切太美妙，簡直不像真實生活。我想，我們一家最大的特點，就是熱情吧！爸爸的熱情表現在科學，媽媽用筆，我則用設計，哥哥呢！嗯，他最棒，他

有我們全家所具有的熱情——科學、筆,和思考。」在淚眼中,我再讀下去:「媽媽,謝謝您把您的寫作世界分享給我,在臺灣短短假期是我最難忘的經驗。幸好您堅持我學中文。」

　　想像著你一邊喝茶,一邊懷念臺北,一邊寫信的情景,難忘你八歲那年,與哥哥一起回臺北度暑假,有一天晚上你告訴我:「媽媽,我覺得好奇怪,我看到路上那麼多和我一樣黑頭髮黑眼睛的人,我的鼻子怎麼酸酸的?」我把你摟在懷裡。是怎麼樣的懷抱孕育出的孩兒。我已然明白,你,不是一個只會頑皮淘氣的小男生而已,你已經開始觀察並加以思考,這正是我們最希望給予你的能力。

　　回學校後,你說開始愛上喝茶,以前,你是只喝可樂與冰水的,看著你的信,我忍不住要喝采,哈,你的飲食文化水平提高了,恭喜你嘍。對於你,東方西方都是一樣,但是多一份了解與欣賞,我們的心胸就多一些空間,也就不會用偏狹的氣度去批判了。

　　兒時扭著身子拒絕上中文學校的小子,現在正經八百的向媽媽道謝了。我也就不客氣的收下了。又再一次證明,你們的潛力無窮,有待繼續開發呵!

　　　愛你的媽

■ 慶祝的心情

親愛的女兒：

　　在畢業的季節，到處是畢業的慶典，謝師、歡送會。在每一個關心兒女教育的家庭，這是一年中的大事呢！

　　不論是從幼稚園、小學、中學或大學，結束了一段學業，又開始走向人生的新里程，心中必定是充滿了興奮與歡欣，我好像也感染到了這份慶祝的心情，不僅孩子本人，我想做為父母、師長的更是高興。

　　記得你托兒所畢業的時候，每個人都戴著小小的方帽，還拿到小小的文憑，你們還表演了室內馬戲班，每個人打扮成老虎、獅子、猴子，同樂唱歌。老師忙著為你們拍照，家長忙著鼓掌，我問你開不開心，你當時傻乎乎的回答我：「上學真好玩，我不想畢業。」那時你才四歲半，托兒所之後，就入了幼稚園，天天念著上學真好玩的事，因為學校裡有好多朋友，好多新鮮的事，和爸媽一起，當然沒有那麼多新奇變化。從幼稚園到高中畢業，一路學習。那個害羞的，握著爸媽不放的小手，開始掙脫了大手走自己的路，不再依賴無助；那個每晚要念故事書才能入睡的小孩，急著要

自己也念一段表現表現……每一個步伐都是一個變化、一個成長，作為父母的是多麼高興你們這樣一步步的走向獨立的人格。

我們在成長的階段，都有許多的憧憬和夢想，你小時候看救火車，好神氣，立志要當救火員。後來又要當蝙蝠俠、米老鼠，上學後，一下子要做小狗的醫生，一下子又要做垃圾工人……從你的日新月異，時時變化的志願中，你也慢慢的認識了自己，關心到周圍的事物，這一切都是從學習中得來的。

每一個夢想的實現，都必須有許多的腳踏實地的行動，否則也只是夢想而已。畢業是學業的一個段落，也正是檢視自己成果的時候，每一個成果，都是付出的收穫，我們盡了心，學習到知識技能，多麼值得慶賀。其實，不必等到畢業，每天做成一件事，用心盡力完成的事，都要為自己加油祝賀。畢業，就是學業的總校閱，再一次的給自己一個回顧反思的機會。我知道你正朝這個方向前進，我在此祝福你，也祝賀完成學業的孩子，這是一個值得慶祝的日子，為你們自己的學習和成長，恭喜你們。

愛你的媽

■ 上網路要小心

親愛的江兒：

　　要感謝科技的發達，我們可以常常在電子郵件上通話，雖然臺灣和美國之間隔了太平洋，我們還是可以有許多內心的交流，無形中縮短了空間的距離。有時候，寫信比交談更能深入，因為語言不能表達的心裡感覺，文字很容易就傳遞了，所以我一直寫作，也正是對文字有深切的感情之故。

　　你在信上提到有些人利用資訊高速公路，可以坐在家裡，而和世界各地的人聊天，結交朋友，但是也有人因為在網路上無所不談，而日久生情，甚至掉入「陷阱」。所以提到人與人之間互信的問題。

　　你的問題正好是我最近一直想和年輕的朋友一起討論的，因為上網路不必有見面的壓力，對於內向害羞的人，很有吸引力，可以整天面對著螢幕，而足不出戶。有些不肖之徒及投機商人，已經利用青少年的好奇、天真，時有不法的行為或騷擾出現，我們正好提出來與大家討論，尤其是暑假期

間，喜歡躲在房中上網路的孩子，更要提高警覺。

要注意的事項有——

1.不要將家中的住址、電話、學校名稱、私人資料隨便告訴別人。如果想和朋友通信、交換照片，一定要讓父母明瞭狀況，或商量見面場合。

2.遇到有色情暴力的語言或圖片，不予理會，並且要告知父母，或留下拷貝，由父母寄給訂購公司抗議。

3.遇到困難狀況，如對方談及隱私、打擊、痛苦事件……，應與父母商量，不要自己承擔這些煩惱。

人與人之間，本來是應該互相尊重，互相信賴的，但是自從資訊爆炸之後，千奇百怪的事都會發生，使人與人之間，充滿了疏離與不信任，多麼可悲！在美國你也聽說過，一個自稱年輕的少女，可能是半老的男子；一個熱情想與你交友的人，可能是想賣東西給你的商人。由於一切有幕前與幕後之別，真假虛實，也全憑想像，上網路的危險，不是開車在路上的橫衝直撞出車禍，而是被騷擾、被侵犯隱私的不安寧。

但是，千萬別因此而忽略了在網路上可以學習的機會，多利用科技的方便，欣賞科學的新知，譬如人類上了月球，現在又探視了火星的奇妙世界，這是多麼偉大的成就。唯有

會利用機會，充實自己的人，機會才會不斷產生，而學習的
樂趣也就層出不窮。也許你們將來有機會上月球，去火星旅
遊，多多充實自己的知識，正是時候。等機會來了，才不會
失之交臂，錯失良機。

愛你的媽

■ 學會保護自己

親愛的莉兒：

最近常常與家長們做親子教育講習 (Workshop)，許許多多的親子問題都提出來討論，尤其是有女兒的媽媽們，更是提心吊膽，什麼性騷擾，強暴案……一切可怕的事例，使活著的樂趣全消失了。而最後，他們會以一種羨慕的口吻對著沒有女兒的父母說：

「多好，你們不用擔心，男孩子比較安全。」

是嗎？

你覺得我們對待男孩、女孩應該有不同的標準嗎？根據美國司法部一九九〇年的調查報告統計，每四名女孩就有一名會遭受性攻擊（騷擾），同資料顯示每六名男孩就有一名遭受性攻擊。所以男孩女孩都要學會保護自己。記得美國各中小學，都有指導孩子保護自己，應付騷擾的方法，碰到有人輕浮或不尊重時，給予糾正。譬如說：

1.「我不喜歡你這種騷擾的行為。」口氣堅定，直接了當。但表情嚴肅，不帶笑容。不論男孩女孩，若有人出言不遜，或有心騷擾占便宜，他就會心裡有數，惡意不得逞，以後再不敢隨意欺侮別人。敢說出自己感覺，自尊尊人是第一步。

2.記錄日期、地點及對方所用字眼。可為來日做有力證據，雖然不必過分緊張，但溫和堅定要從小養成。

3.向父母、師長或朋友同學說明經過。

4.讓對方明白犯錯要道歉或受罰。不必想太多替對方脫罪或給予模糊的訊息，以為你不在意就隨意占便宜。

保護個人的基本權利，是要從小就培養的，不僅自己要免於受到騷擾，也要尊重別人，不要去侵犯別人。小學生或半大不小的孩子，有時淘氣，常常逗弄同學，去年發生在北卡州的一年級小男生，因逗弄同班女同學，被學校以「性騷擾」罪名處罰，大概也是因為大多數頑皮的孩子，不知尊重別人，以為拉拉辮子，把女同學氣哭是很好玩的事。我曾經和你以及許多大孩子討論此事，一致的看法也認為中小學裡，是有些愛捉弄人的人，對於這種侵犯他人的行為，要及早阻止，以免長大了「討人嫌」或更有甚者，變成騷擾他人或攻擊別人的罪行。

　　媽媽從小就要你們自尊尊人，因為唯有從尊重中，人與人的關懷才會滋長，社會的和諧才會形成風氣。我願在此深深祝福你們，將來生存的空間充滿和諧與尊重。

愛你的媽

後記

親愛的媽媽，

現在是六月中，雨季已經悄悄來到了日本。早晨的通勤人潮，擠滿著身穿合身黑西裝的上班族，匆忙穿越溼漉漉的街道，趕往附近的車站。車廂內，每個人互相推擠著，急於穿越擁擠的人群和沈重的溼氣，搶坐最後一個座位。

在這樣的情況下，可以想見大家的臉上是很難保持笑容的。有時候，空氣太過沈重，人群太過擁擠，連要抬起自己的視線都很困難；然而，我仍試著保持樂觀愉悅的心情，珍惜能在這裡體驗如此不同的文化和生活方式的機會。

回想起上次我們之間的通信，那時正是我還在加州念書，而您和爸爸人在臺灣的時候。當時，我從沒想到過我的工作，會帶著我由美國前往歐洲，接著又來到日本。我當然很感激能得到這樣的機會，卻也對人生境遇的轉折感到有些吃驚。

我想，無論在任何時候，人都很難看出自己的人生會走向何方。但是，我從您和爸爸身上學到，只要時機一到，盡心盡力做到最好，我們自然會被帶往下個階段，而下一個機會也就隨之出現了。即使是在我不知道該如何往下走，或不知道會往哪裡去的時候，這個道理也依然真確；雖然專注在完成手邊的工作，但是在這個過程中，盡最大的努力、付出自己的所有，這本身已經儼然是我的目標了。所以過程本身就成了目標，而其餘的部分將會水到渠成。

當我停下腳步，暫時跳出每日的繁忙，去思考——就像您教過我的一樣——明白自己到過的地方和人生給予我的東西時，我很高興的發現，我一直都是跟隨著人生的轉變，卻依然忠於自己的道路。就像您曾引用神學家坎伯說的那句名言：「英雄的旅程乃是找到他自己的途徑。」而這，也許就是追求任何事物最根本的道理。

這樣的追求過程帶領我到了許多不可思議的地方，接觸到許多不平凡的人物與經驗。這一切給了我許多幫助——也讓我信任自己所走的路是對的，更學會知足——這比什麼都要可貴。

我很感謝您和爸爸藉由鼓勵我順著人生暗藏的驚喜，追求對我有意義的人生道路，而讓我學會了要對生活感到知足。只要想到這裡，我就能忽略早晨電車上擠在我身旁的通勤人潮，對外面綿綿陰雨不以為意，而露出笑容。

從日本，
愛您的廷兒
2004 年 6 月 12 日

親愛的 Jane,

　　看到妳稱呼我為妳的「老師」時，讓我忍不住會心一笑，並回想起 1978 年我們在北卡州立大學相遇的那天。當時的妳，是個充滿熱誠的年輕媽媽，急於想成為圖書館學系的研究生。當我聽到妳的故事、又談起寫作，看到妳眼中所閃耀的光芒時，我用一種近似冒失而激動的態度告訴妳：「Jane,妳註定該寫書，而不是進入圖書館系，學習圖書管理!」

　　我在北卡州立大學任教的第一年，妳和從英國來的 Michael Chalmers 一起參與了我的工作，成為我全職的工作搭檔。我們系上的一位南方女祕書，常常說她完全無法聽懂我們在說什麼，因為我們的談話充滿不同的腔調!

　　我們在實地研究做了很好的工作，好些鮮為人知的成人才開始學習讀和寫，他們（所謂的「文盲」）也受我們邀稿，寫出他們的故事，妳的工作出色的表現在碩士論文考試那天，考試委員會深受感動，正如我早有同感。

　　妳的孩子們長大了，妳先生的事業有了成就，並將北卡州立大學介紹給中國大陸而建立交流。我也創辦了「朱伯利成人教育中心」，到世界各地進行教學的工作。

　　我們一起在洛麗創辦了「中華文教中心」（後更名為簡宛

文教中心），希望能將東方文化之美傳授給美國南方人。而妳不僅在專業領域上展現了光芒，之後更在出書與寫作方面有了亮眼的成績。我們常說要一起合作寫書；這樣的機會，在妳說到有意將《給愛兒的二十封信》改編成中英雙語版本時，終於出現了。於是我們通力合作，一起將妳的中文散文翻譯成英文。

我想等我上了天堂以後，第一件要做的事就是要求能閱讀妳作品的原文——中文！我明白即使是這樣一本簡單的書，我們還是無法盡善盡美的詮釋出妳的原文。中文的措辭之美、文章的節奏和韻律、以及譬喻裡隱含的細微差異等等，英文版本仍然無法完全捕捉到其精髓。

然而，這仍然是一次讓我引以為傲的合作經驗，它也證明了一件我一直以來都明白的事——妳真是我的良師！我的益友！

謝謝妳！

Jane

Letters to My Son

■ Happy New Year Across the Miles

Dear Tim:

Dad and I finally arrived in Taipei!

Being in Taiwan for Chinese New Year has been our dream for over twenty years. You can well imagine how happy we are to finally be home for this year's holiday!

Naturally, there were crowds at the Taipei airport: families and relatives rushing home for their own celebrations. For us, though, just being in Taiwan again was enough to make us happy. The long lines waiting before rows of immigration cubicles did not bother us a bit.

Much like heading home for Christmas in the US, all the inconveniences of traveling—delayed flights, sometimes even spending the night in an airport—were overshadowed by the main reason for the trip: the happiness to be with one's family. The joyous reunion in sight makes almost anything bearable. It puts everybody in a good mood no matter how frustrating the situation at hand gets to be.

In a sense, I found that if one faces a bad situation with an upbeat mood, the situation could change character and turn out to be not so bad after all. As a matter of fact, it was you and your brother who taught me that lesson. When you used to fly home for Christmas every year, amidst the chaos of holiday traveling, you never complained about crowded airports or delayed flights. Ever since you were a little boy, you've felt that there was no use getting upset. You would say, "What good does it do if you get excited?" Then, with a sketchbook in hand, you would pass time sketching an automobile or the people around you. You were always so "cool" in unpleasant situations.

But when you were younger, this "I don't care" temperament really bothered me. You always followed your own way of doing things—you never throw tantrums, but you did not let us lead you by the nose. You were always independent-minded and did things your own way: on school days, you got up when you wanted to, and as for homework, you did everything on your own plan. Now whenever I bragged about my giving you good study habits, your tongue-in-cheek reply would be, "I'm just glad that you never forced me to study."

Well, your father and I had to apply some of your "cool" attitude on this trip to Taiwan, except that we did not bring a sketchbook and crayons. Not only was the airport overcrowded, but the airline somehow managed to lose our luggage as well. Upon hearing the bad news, Dad simply said, "No problem, just deliver the bags when they arrive." Without a fuss, we left the airport. Your uncle came with a big car for the luggage to meet us. Too bad we had to disappoint him!

Everywhere in Taipei, Chinese New Year is in the air, although much less so than the time when we were young. There are no firecrackers, and no lanterns or buntings. Still, it feels different than in the United States. Over there, Christmas and Thanksgiving are the important holidays in every family. In the United States, Chinese New Year comes at the time when you still had to go to school, and we still had to go to work. That was why I always tried to talk about Chinese traditions and culture at home and even in your school, sometimes allowing you to invite friends to our house to share in the experience.

That was how we cultivated your sense of Chinese customs and traditions. Of course, the "New Year money" became the part you and your brother loved most. After our arrival in

Taipei, your brother called to say, "Daddy and Mommy, gong-xi-fa-cai, hong-bao-na-lai." (In other words, "May you have a prosperous New Year. Now, where is my red envelope?")

This year, the four of us are separated in three different places. Do you still remember the Chinese poem I taught you, "One caring heart is the same, even in five different places?" Come to think of it, it has been like this since you and your brother entered college.

Confucius once said that "one does not leave home when the parents remain there." Nowadays, technology helps us stay in touch in a shrinking world. Our motto has become "we'll run around the world together." It is our experience of growing up together as a family that will always keep us close, no matter the distance.

So from our home, your home, in every corner of this world, let us wish each other a very happy and prosperous Chinese New Year. May you have good health, and may everything go well for each one of us this year.

Love,
Mom

■ Between Old and New

Dear Tim:

I awoke this morning to find out that Taipei was in the midst of a drizzle. Taipei during Chinese New Year is surprisingly quiet, because there are fewer cars and no firecrackers. I stood by the window, looking down the street. My thoughts were about you and your brother, and my own childhood growing up in Taiwan.

Back then, we used to look forward to Chinese New Year. Our greatest anticipation was the chance to wear new clothes and new shoes. In those days, children received new clothing only once every year. Your grandmother was both resourceful and adept with her hands, often altering adult's clothes for her children. Likewise, shoes were only purchased when the previous pair were truly worn out, which was not very often. Thus, Chinese New Year was the only time we truly had brand-new clothes. When I was in high school, it was my responsibility, as the eldest sibling, to take the younger ones to Taipei to buy new clothes and new shoes. This annual outing was really a "big deal" for all of us.

In those days, the town of Chung-He was rather a remote place with no bus service. Pedicabs were only available after crossing Hua-Jiang Bridge, so much of the trip was made on foot. Still, that never seemed to bother us. In fact, we often invited friends to go with us, turning it into a fun "field trip" for the day.

It's funny that I remember the pleasure of new clothes so clearly. The fear of scarcity and poverty that surrounded us then have slowly faded away with time. When I recall my childhood in Chung-He, I am filled with warm sweet memories. Why is it so, you might ask? We had no television, no toys, and no modern appliances. How could we still be so happy? I know it is hard to imagine.

But yes, we were happy. Do you know why? We children always felt safe, loved, and cared for at home. That's why. That sounds hard to believe, but it's absolutely true. In addition, we had active imagination! We used to pretend that a stick of bamboo was a horse that we "rode" by dragging it along between our legs. We would imagine that freshly peeled grapefruit skins were precious pork—the pinkish part of the skin were lean meat, the white part were the fat. We would pretend to weigh it with a hand scale, which was just a chopstick, and then "sold" the meat like a butcher in the market. Or, we made a small tent under the altar table, pretending that it were our little house. You did much the same thing when you were young, do you still remember?

Ah, childhood life, it's all fun play without pressure. The world was unlimited! If we became hungry or thirsty from our games, there was always someone at home to look after us. Home was never just an empty house with toys and a television set. Of course, if we stayed out for too long or too late, my parents would scold us. It was not fun to be scolded, but it also became sweet in recollection, because we were loved and cared about. Now your grandpa and grandma are gone, but I miss their scolding. Their caring and loving are always in my heart.

I've often told you that new clothes and toys can be bought, but they are not the most important things. There are things that cost nothing but are more important to be cherished forever. You didn't always understand this when you were young. You

liked wearing name brands like everyone else in high school. I taught you the Chinese idiom, "Judge a good horse not by its hair color." You responded that, "But it would be even better if good horses also had a good hair color!"

What you said gave me reason to pause. While a good horse that also had a good color would be nice, it is still the inner strength of the horse that should be valued more than its appearance. As you came to understand the importance of individual quality and being yourself, you were no longer so attached to those name brands. You have grown up!

While new clothes and shoes can make one happy, it is those things that are passed down and become part of your childhood and memory that are truly valuable.

During this Chinese New Year, I can't help but reflect on the past because it reminds me of the most precious things in my life. What about you? What precious memories do you reflect upon at this time of year?

Love,
Mom

■ Remembering My Childhood

Dear Tim:

I woke up this morning to the smiling face of a bright sun. Quickly putting on my running shoes, I went out for a jog.

Still waiting for our luggage to arrive, we are staying at your uncle's home, the place where I spent my childhood. I took a walk to my former elementary school, and couldn't resist going inside to take a look. Your aunts, uncles and I all graduated from this school, and we still harbor a great deal of nostalgia for it.

The school has changed. Many new buildings have been added over the years. There is now less open space. As the morning breeze brushed softly across my face, I stood in the playground, with childhood memories

flooding my mind. This is the place where I used to play dodge ball and tug-of-war, and where I learned to ride a bike. All memories flew before my eyes.

During my elementary school years, society was simple, and we lived a frugal life. In remote villages like ours, many of my classmates came to school without shoes. I envied my barefooted classmates because, during our lunch break, they could play in a nearby pond. They would go right into the water to chase the fish!

I remember that one day, I was tired of watching and decided to take off my shoes and socks to join them. Unfortunately, I fell in the pond! My clothes were all wet and some broken glass cut my foot badly. I was really a mess. When I returned home after school, your grandfather punished me to stand in the corner facing the wall all afternoon. I learned my lesson that day: when I did not obey the rules, the Heavens as well as my parents would punish me! I felt so guilty that I never dared to go barefoot into that pond again.

Back then, our class had more than fifty students aged

between 8 and 12, and all of the teachers were very strict. No one was allowed to leave the room during class or to move about. Many first graders would wet their pants in the classroom because they were too scared to ask for permission to go to the bathroom. A few still could not control themselves in the second or third grade. Years later, when I took the course of Educational Psychology in college, this problem was discussed during a class session. The consensus was that very young children do not always have physical self-control, especially if they are nervous or in a new environment. Hopefully elementary school students in Taiwan today are not bound by such strict rules anymore.

The classroom environment was so different in America when you went to grade school. Each class had two teachers and only 20-plus pupils. When I volunteered as a teacher's assistant there, I felt exhausted after a few hours by those little boys and girls who were full of energy. Compared with American children, Chinese children were perhaps too passive, quiet and obedient. I often think how nice it would be if one could find the

balance between the discipline of the East and the vitality of the West.

I pondered this as I left my old school's campus. The morning sun shone on the school children as they arrived for their classes with schoolbags on their back. They greeted me with polite, smiling faces. Young student "police" were helping to direct traffic as their schoolmates crossed the road. Hope and happiness permeated the air as I walked the familiar route again. My heart was filled with joy and optimism as I watched these young people, thinking of their bright future while reflecting on my own happy past.

Love,
Mom

■ The Pleasures of Hiking

Dear Tim:

We've moved into our new home.

It is located in Nan-Kang, the northeastern part of Taipei, at the foot of small hills. When the weather is fine, we can climb to the top of one of those hills to have Taipei city before our eyes. The view is magnificent.

Having lived in the east coast of America for so long, I missed the fun of hiking through hills and valleys. In the eastern part of the United States, there are geologically old formations, like Appalachian Mountains. West of these are the central plains. Only further west does one encounter the Rocky Mountains, in size and grandeur very different from the East coast. In fact, two-thirds of the land of Taiwan is mountainous, and ever since my teenage years, I have enjoyed exploring its natural terrain.

Because there are hills and scenic views everywhere, I tried not to miss any opportunity for hiking in Taipei. In suburban

Taipei, you run into morning hikers everywhere, every day. Soon after daybreak, hordes of people, old and young, crowd the foothills and open spaces, to breathe fresh air and listen to chirping birds. In and around Nan-Kang, one can take a short thirty-minute hike, or head for higher mountains in a three-hour trip. From one hill to another, one can even take the bus back. Your aunt Celia and I took every opportunity to do some hiking in the area.

It's a pity that you and your brother did not have more opportunities to do some mountain exploring of your own, as you were growing up in North Carolina. From where we live, Great Smoky Mountains National Park is five hours away by car. Do you remember when the family went camping in Mt. Pisgah and Mt. Mitchell when you were young? Sometimes Dad would take you and your brother skiing in those mountains as part of 4-H Club activities. Even though I enjoy hiking, camping was not my favorite sport, and I was afraid of breaking a bone while skiing. That probably kept us from more frequent trips to the Smoky Mountains.

There was a good reason for my aversion towards camping. When we first arrived in the United States, before you were born and while Giles was still just a toddler, we went to the Thousand Islands in northern New York State on a camping trip with friends from Cornell. At the beginning, we all had a good time. We set up tents, sang songs, and barbecued meat over a camp fire. However, just around midnight it started to rain. It poured for hours and the temperature kept dropping. We were so worried that Giles might catch a cold. We brought him into the car, turned on the heater, but then began to worry about how long the car battery might last! By morning, when the rain finally stopped, we were all exhausted. Through it all your brother slept peacefully like an angel. Nonetheless, I became wary of camping ever since, and fussed over blankets and rainproof equipment whenever the subject came up. That was why we usually opted for warmer beach vacations over more camping adventures.

Now that I'm back in Taiwan, where two-thirds of land is mountainous, I look forward to mountain hiking like the ones I

used to enjoy when I was young. In college years my favorite pastime was mountain climbing. When you come to Taipei next time, I shall take you to hike the hills around Taipei .

"To look at the world from a high vantage point" is to change one's outlook on life. That was what Confucius meant when he mused that, "one's view of the world changes from atop Mount Tai." With a view from the top of any mountain, we realize how small and insignificant we really are. That is the way to avoid a "frog's view from the bottom of a well." I want you to learn this habit of mountain climbing to acquire a broader view of the world.

Even as I write, the mountains outside are beckoning. Until the next time.

Love,
Mom

■ Making Your Dream Come True

Dear Tim:

How are you?

Dad and I went to a health club yesterday. You know that Dad loves to swim. When he saw the indoor pool, he signed up as a member right away. Today, he went to swim, without wasting a single day. I am not much of a swimmer. I prefer rhythmic calisthenics and aerobics. I have no interest nor aptitude for track and field, nor any kind of ball game. Call it what you like, but the root of that "repulsion" comes from a bad experience I had when I was young.

When I was a child, I fell accidentally into the water and had to be rescued. It was a very traumatic experience. In those days, not many people could swim. As a child, I constantly heard stories of some children who drowned while playing in the river. I was told that they were taken away by the ghosts of victims who drowned in the same locale a long time ago. Horror stories like these instilled in me a kind of aversion toward swimming. It is amazing how such childhood fears could stay with me. Until I was twenty, I would panic whenever I was near water.

Of course, now that I know a little about psychology, I realize that this is a phobia that can be overcome. When you and your brother were young, I never wanted to influence both of you with my fear of water. I confronted my phobia by enrolling with you and Giles in swimming lessons at the YMCA. It was not easy for me to be in the water with you, but I did it and proved that you can, indeed, "teach an old dog new tricks!"

Learning to swim came naturally for both of you. While I was able to overcome my fear of water, I only managed more or less to float in the water, not really swim. Still, I was a good pool-side cheerleader, watching you and Giles swim, applauding every little improvement in your style or technique. I always felt so proud just sitting by the pool, because you two were such good swimmers.

Watching your dad swim in the club's heated pool yesterday, I wish I could be a carefree fish! In reality, I have to stand up to take a breath after a few strokes. My pleasure of swimming gave way to the thought of forced labor, killing the fun altogether.

This is what "self-imposed limits" do to a person. Fear, mixed with lack of confidence and will, can often bar us from truly fulfilling our dreams. Childhood shadows tend to stay with us; if we do not overcome them, they become a roadblock, turning heavier and harder to remove as we get older.

This reminds me of the time when we were in the United States, a friend decided to join the "flyers' club," precisely because he was terrified of traveling by air. After he learned all about airplanes and flying, he understood how everything works, and could face traveling by air confidently.

I am sharing my experience with you, so that whenever you feel any anxiety or lack of confidence, face it by finding out the cause of your fear and understand the reasons. By facing the problem head-on, you can overcome your fear sooner and restore your self-confidence. That is no different than finding your way in total darkness. If you had some idea of where

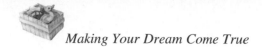

you're heading for, consulted a map and knew the direction, you would not be afraid of the darkness at all. Isn't that so?

Remember, next time when you're afraid of something, face it and try to understand it, then nothing will stand in your way, and your dreams will come true.

Love,
Mom

■ Fun with Books

Dear Tim:

It was a great day today.

After so many rainy days, the sun finally came out. I walked into the Academia Sinica campus which was quiet and peaceful, away from the traffic noise outside. I passed many buildings until I finally found the library. You know that I've always been a lover of books. I was delighted to have a full year to explore this treasure trove of not just books and periodicals, but also academic journals and research reports.

Speaking of books and libraries, I was reminded of the time when you used to accompany me to the library every day. You were just over two years old then, while I was taking a children's literature course at the University of Illinois. Every week I had hundreds of children's books to read and write reports on. I always took you with me when I went to the library to study.

You carried a miniature backpack, containing not

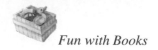
notebooks, but crayons and a drawing pad. When you got tired of reading picture books, you would take out the crayons and start drawing. A child's attention span is rather limited, and you would soon walk over to the drinking fountain to take a sip of water.

The librarians knew how young you were, and being impressed with your good behavior, they were always generous with praise. The more they praised you, the better you behaved. You would put your little finger to your lips when other children made any noise. "Shhh..." you would say to them. I still remember the expression of your lovely little face.

I believe that the habit of reading comes from one's early experiences. Though you were too young to read at that time, being around books made you feel comfortable enough to pick out those colorful toddlers' books. Your favorite one was a

picture book called "Little Blue and Little Yellow" by Leo Lionni. I read it to you at least ten times, so you could recite the whole book along with me. But you still insisted on hearing more of it again and again.

One day, when my good friends "Aunt Yellow" and "Aunt Blue" (that was what their surnames meant in Chinese) came to our house to visit, you stared at them and insisted that they hug each other. Nobody understood why, but they cheerfully obliged. Then, with a puzzled look, you asked, "Why didn't Aunt Yellow and Aunt Blue turn into Aunt Green?" We all laughed so hard that we almost fell from our chairs.

I had to explain to my friends about your favorite book, "Little Blue and Little Yellow." When Yellow and Blue touched each other, they turned Green in color. I think your sense of color was sharpened by reading Leo Lionni's book, and you started to draw with all kinds of colors ever since.

Ah, that was so many years ago. I must have missed you so much today that I could not help recalling such memories from your childhood. Now you are grown up, and on your own in

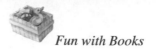

America. Did you celebrate Chinese New Year where you are? Maybe you missed the chance to have a proper Chinese meal in Chinatown to mark the occasion. Hopefully next year you will be in Taiwan for the New Year, and the whole family can enjoy an authentic Chinese dinner together. I look forward to it.

Love,
Mom

■ Self-Esteem

Dear Tim:

Your letter has just arrived.

In it you asked about "self-esteem," and whether the Chinese characters have the same connotation as in English. I'm so glad that you have become interested in comparing the two languages. Do you remember the year you came to Taiwan to study Chinese at the Language Center of The Mandarin Daily News? You were very reluctant at the beginning. If you had not met some good friends and a good teacher who coached you patiently, you might have become a real "banana" as people say. That is, yellow on the outside but all white inside, the somewhat derogatory term for those American-born Chinese, who only look Chinese but don't have the faintest idea about their cultural roots.

Yes, I believe "self-esteem" in Chinese means almost the same as in English. Everybody should have self-esteem, though that should not be confused with arrogance. During adolescence,

young people frequently experience sudden shift in moods, one moment they would feel happy and exuberant, the next moment moody and withdrawn. Can you recall this period of your life?

Those who have self-esteem always act on their own initiative with a sense of honor and responsibility. They do not shy away from difficulties. Those who do not have self-esteem, on the other hand, tend to be negative and complain frequently. Lacking initiative, they are more easily led by others and more likely to give up when faced with challenges.

Take learning Chinese for instance. The second generation Chinese living abroad, like you, never consider learning their parents' mother tongue as easy and natural. Many would give up at the end; some persisted and succeeded. Those who gave up always say, it's too difficult, or what's the use of it anyway? But there are always some who doggedly carry on, because they believe that if others could do it, so could they.

Between "can do" and "difficult to do," it's all in one's mind. Young children do not understand that success or failure is more a matter of attitude than anything else. Self-esteem determines one's attitude, which is largely dependent on parents and teachers. If your parents were always saying "You are so dumb!" or "Why can't you even learn such a simple matter?" or your teacher scolds you daily and calls you a poor student, you would be so frustrated and gradually lose your self-esteem. You could start to believe what they are telling you that you really are inferior to others. "I am so dumb!" It is a simple self-proclaimed death sentence. What a shame that could be!

You are lucky to have had good teachers who recognized and encouraged you at school all the way. It naturally followed that we as your parents had little to worry about while you were growing up. For this reason, I often tell my friends not to scold their children. I also tell other children not to be discouraged or think of themselves as inferior. Who will love you if you do not love yourself?

You know that Dad and I love you and your brother very much. Even if we might have unknowingly hurt your pride on occasion, both of you always remained confident and you liked to declare, "I am who I am."

That was great, because you are yourself and nobody else. You have your character which is unique and worthy of respect. Your self-confidence gives you the ability to respect others, and earn respect from them. That is something you have to cultivate from childhood. Your father and I do respect you, and hope that your healthy self-esteem continues to grow with you throughout your life.

Love,
Mom

■ Memories of the Attic

Dear Tim:

Do you remember my old home that I spoke about so many times, the house where I was born? It was built before I was born, and I lived there until I married your father. You can imagine how attached I am to it. I cherish its memory with all my heart.

This old house has a very high ceiling, and was built with steel and concrete. The outside, covered by white ceramic tiles, was quite stylish at that time. I remember that when we were little, anytime there was an earthquake, neighbors would come to our home for shelter. They reasoned that our house would certainly be able to withstand the tremors without collapsing.

My favorite childhood hiding place was the attic. When my siblings and I played hide-and-seek, it was always a great place to hide! It was always dark up there. Only a little sunlight would come through the small skylight, creating a soft poetic ring of light on the floor. I remember reading Little Women when I was

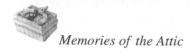

in junior high and finding out that Jo locked herself in her attic every day to write her stories. I often imagined myself locked in the attic of our old house, enjoying my daydreams there.

I always had to share a room with my siblings. How I wished that I had had a corner of my own in the attic! Unfortunately, with so little light in the attic though, my fantasy of staying there to write never came into being.

So many years have passed since those childhood fantasies. As I stood in the attic recently, with the circle of sunlight still sneaking in, I could see mementoes around me bringing my childhood days back to me. Along the wall, I saw the tiny millstone and cake molds. The millstone is for grinding glutinous rice which, when cooked and mixed with other ingredients, is used to make traditional rice cakes. We especially enjoyed making the "red turtle cake," shaped like a turtle and colored by red food dye. The process is not so different from working with the "Play Dough" you know from your childhood. On

the wall also hung a coolie hat and a coir rain coat, both made from Chinese coir palm. Those were the traditional rainwear for farmers. They are antiques now, but you probably have never seen them before. I shall have to show them to you when you come to the old house again.

I was very touched to see our school yearbooks and classroom notes, neatly packed and organized into boxes and crates, each clearly labeled with your grandmother's handwriting. I didn't realize that she had organized the scattered papers and photographs of her seven children before she passed away. My tears fell freely as I flipped through the pages of memories. I miss my mother very, very much.

The boxes and crates reminded me of how, during your home visit on Christmas, we organized our own things back in North Carolina before leaving for Taiwan. You saw the things I had kept for you — stationery items, awards and commendations, your first drawing, even your first baby tooth. You laughed at that and called me "sentimental." I guess all parents are alike in that way. We cherish even the smallest memories of our beloved children. You will understand that when you become a parent yourself.

Although it might seem sentimental to keep a son's or daughter's memorabilia all those years, a child who grows up with that kind of love and attention will also be imbued with a sense of encouragement. Hopefully, you will look back on your own childhood the same way, and pass on that same love and attention to those around you.

Back in the attic, with the tiny circle of light on the floor, my memories are still accumulating through the seasons and through the years, much like the love in my heart, deep-rooted and still blooming.

Mom misses you, dear Tim.

Love,
Mom

■ Never Underestimate Yourself

Dear Tim:

This morning I took a public bus in Taipei, and noticed it still is full of school children. There have been, of course, quite some changes compared to the buses we rode to school years ago. Because there are more buses and more routes, today's buses are not nearly as crowded as they used to be. Back then, we were really packed like sardines in a can; you could hardly fit anything however small in between the passengers.

I sat next to a group of students chatting amongst themselves. I asked what grade they were in, and they said they were in the third year of junior high, equivalent to the 8th grade in the United States. Their conversation was solely about the upcoming final examinations. They expressed doubts about their own intelligence and ability to score well. I could sense their abjection and lack of confidence in their future.

It made me wonder what kind of huge burden teenagers in Taiwan bear today. I do not remember that you carried such loads or had similar worries during your teenage years. You joined a soccer team, played piano, took art classes, and were kept busy all the time. You even formed a dance crew with your friends and won some talent shows. But I do remember that at the same age as these students, you did have some doubts and you were not so sure of yourself.

Maybe you thought you were not muscular enough or handsome enough. Your teeth looked terrible (you were wearing braces at the time). Standing alongside your schoolmates, you did not have their curly hair and high nose bridge, nor could you tell funny jokes. But, you are who you are. Do you remember Mom's encouraging words?

"You are who you are!" That was the confidence pill that Mom kept dosing you with.

Yes, you are who you are. While you do not look like the average American boy, you have your bi-cultural background. You speak both languages. You have your talents—you can draw, you can play soccer, and you can choreograph your own rap dance. A bright future awaits you. How enviable that is!

Is that the right prescription? A positive attitude can relieve you of your worries. Just think of your teachers, parents, brother, aunts and uncles who love and care about you. Well, there are so many of them. You should not put yourself down, or overlook what you can do. There is only one of you in the whole wide world. No more and no less, that's why you are unique.

Of course, teenagers sometimes don't see this for themselves. They worry, sometimes unnecessarily, at that age. As a famous Chinese poet put it, "In youth one has not really tasted sorrow, but writes of sadness only in pretension." And it was for the same adolescent temperament as in "The Sorrows of Young Werther."

Remember, don't pay attention to those things that might make you think less of yourself. But do affirm and strengthen those things that set you apart from the others. The talents and abilities that you are proud of— your dance, your athletic skill, your voice. Let your specialty speak for itself. That will be really "cool," and not just "in," because it cannot be bought with money.

If you fail any exam, there will always be another chance. If you have done your best, that is the best anybody can do. But if you let yourself down in negative thoughts, you will be caught in a cycle of self-doubt and pity. Never underestimate yourself.

Do you agree with Mom's words?

Love,
Mom

■ Creative You

Dear Tim:

    It's raining cats and dogs outside. They say that Taiwan's rainy season is at hand. I stood by the window, looking down on the rainy scene in a sort of stupor. The weather today has changed my plans: I decided to stay home instead of going to the art exhibit as I had hoped because the rain also dampened my spirit.

    From the window, I suddenly spotted a child and his mother walking under a large umbrella. They seemed to be taking their time, even enjoying themselves on a leisurely stroll. From a distance, they looked as if they could be singing a song together under the protection of their large umbrella. How that scene reminds me of the time when you were that age!

    You were just like that child down on the street when you were little. You always enjoyed playing in the rain, or rolling in the snow. I remember that one day we had planned to go for a picnic, but had to cancel our plans because of rain. You were so disappointed that you stood by the window, saying out aloud:

"Rain, rain, go away. Come again some other day.

I want to go out and play, but I can't have my way.

Mommy won't let me out 'cause she is afraid.

So please, please stop, and come again another day!"

Looking at your cute but sad little face, I was forced to change my mind. I took an umbrella in one hand and your little hand in the other, and together we headed out into the rain. It was your childish innocence that changed my mind, maybe even opened my heart that had become set in its ways. Your imagination and free spirit helped me find pleasure and joy; and I rediscovered fun and innocence, even on a rainy day.

Through your child's view of the world, I was reminded of my own youth and carefree years. Adults often worry too much and carry around too many taboos, causing them to act withdrawn and defensive at times. I always hoped that this would not happen to you and you could always keep your imagination and free spirit intact, allowing your optimism and happy nature to continue to flourish.

But as you grew up and reached adolescence, you seemed to be losing your confidence too. This self-doubt became more pronounced when you became a teenager. You were at times almost negative and uncertain of your feelings. Fortunately though, you found new balance through your carefree nature, which carried you through your doubtful times.

Your natural talent in drawing, dancing and even dressing differently became your creative outlets, ways to express your inner thoughts and passions. Your individuality and creativity also came out in other ways, which your father and I tried not to judge by stereotyped values. We learned to live with them, rather than criticizing them through traditional eyes.

Do you remember when you grew a braid of long hair? That "rat tail" was quite unique for boys at 10 to 12 years of age. Soon afterwards though, when it became quite fashionable and others also let their hair grew long, you cut your hair short. You also cut off the sleeves of Dad's dress shirts to wear them to class. They looked very saggy to me but earned you a reputation as the most stylish among your peers according to your high school yearbook.

Before the L.A. Boyz became a popular group in Taiwan, you were already dancing with a group of your best friends at home, practically wearing out our living room floor carpet! Your group was even featured on the local TV station. After you had fun, you and dancing friends went on to college with scholarships, turning down more TV appearances. You said, "We're going to college to study, so no more shows."

Your father and I witnessed all this as you grew up, always appreciating your "cool" style. Your having fun, your crazy behavior, and your emotional ups and downs never interfered with your priorities as a student. At the end of high school, you received a four-year university full scholarship, the highest honor for incoming students. "Not everybody gets that kind of full scholarship," you told me with a touch of pride, "Mom, you can trust me."

Yes, I trust you, Tim. I knew that you were special from the day we played together in the rain. Watching you running and splashing through puddles, I knew that I could not mold you, shape you, or limit you with any traditional rules.

I hope that all mothers can discover their inner-child through the eyes of their children, and that they create memories together that they can also treasure for a lifetime.

Love,
Mom

■ You Are Great!

Dear Tim:

Today, I again rode to town on a bus filled with students. They all looked exhausted after their day at school. I took the initiative to chat with them. Even though they were reluctant and shy at first, they loosened up eventually. Then all of a sudden, a young student blurted out, "We are so busy and feel so tired! I have no idea how to handle so much homework. I'm such a failure!"

I looked at their young faces, so anxious with worries at such a young age. Shouldn't they be leading a happy and carefree life now? Why are they so serious and have lost their

smiles already? It reminded me of your junior high years. You were as busy as these students and did not know how to manage your time either. But, you were busy not because you had to study for tests and exams. You were so busy with extracurricular activities — ball games, socials, music, and partying.

As with most teenagers, you didn't know then how to manage your time either. Without proper planning, it was—and still is — nearly impossible to develop some extracurricular talents or to earn some money through part-time jobs, in addition to meeting the demands of school.

Being busy and feeling pressed for time seem to be the norm for all age groups these days. Normally, youngsters should not have come under the same kind of pressure so early in life. Come to think of it, however, this probably means that it's time for them to bid farewell to childhood, and learn to face their own responsibilities. Management of time and pressure is an important lesson to learn. When one starts to feel the shortage of time, and begins to deal with pressure, he is meeting an important challenge in his growing-up process.

The best way to deal with time and pressure is learning to say "No." Do not even attempt to accomplish everything at once. If you want to join every extracurricular activity, accept

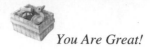

every party invitation, and finish your homework on time, you are biting off more than you can chew. Select a few things you really like to do, then rotate and juggle them well. Imagine someone trying to enjoy all kinds of fun, a TV show, a movie, and other entertainment all at the same time. It is simply impossible to fully enjoy all at the same time.

The beauty of youth is to appreciate and celebrate life. One learns knowledge at school, appreciate warmness from frienship, and joins extracurricular activities to acquire good manners and achieve balance between body and mind. Playing the piano, drawing pictures, or other forms of creativity can also help to expand one's horizon and skills. But remember, you do not have to be number one in all of these. What is truly important is the process of learning. You will always gain more happiness when playing ball games or practicing piano than carrying trophies home. If one only thinks of winning or coming in first, the joy of playing music or the pleasure in sports itself may be lost completely.

Back on the bus, I told the despairing young student, "You

are good! You are not inferior at all!"

Because the most important thing in life is learning to be the master of one's own time, instead of becoming its slave. Do not allow time to push you around, or invite new pressure into your life. Learn to say no, and accept rejection if necessary. If we learn to make our own decisions, we also gain more space and time for ourselves. This is something I have learned throughout the years, and I believe it is worth sharing with you.

Love,
Mom

■ Love and Faith

Dear Tim:

A young student named Kan came to visit me last week. Like most students, he was worried about his homework, his friends, his family, and future. Yesterday, though, he came to see me again and seemed more disturbed than usual.

"What's the matter?" I immediately asked him.

"My parents are fighting again," he told me. "They are always fighting, and now my mom has asked my dad to move out."

"I am sorry to hear that," I tried to console Kan, "If there is anything I can do to help, please let me know."

"Thank you," Kan replied, "I can't talk to my parents about this because they are always fighting with each other or being mad at me, and because I don't invite any classmates home from school, I don't have many friends there either. I don't really know what to do."

I could feel Kan's frustration and it reminded me of a time when you were in the fourth grade and came home worried about your good friend Eric. The first time you came home with that look of concern, you refused to tell me what the matter was.

Some days later, you still wore the same sad face, and finally asked, "Mom, will you and Dad get a divorce? Is our family going to separate?"

"What?" I was shocked. "Why would you ask such a question?"

"Eric's parents are getting divorced, and their family is splitting up!" Tears dropped down your face, showing how worried you were about the same thing happening in our home.

I gave you a hug, dried your tears, and assured you, "Don't worry. Mom and Dad are not getting divorced. Our family will stay together forever."

That was all you needed to hear. Immediately your smile came back like sunshine from behind dark clouds.

Hearing your friends' stories about divorce and separation, you were beginning to think that all families would break up, that there was no use in having faith in family or love. Certainly, if that negativity or doubt was in the air, it would have continued to erode your faith. However, we never would let that happen at home.

Do you remember the book I translated from Leo

Buscaglia, *Living, Loving and Learning*? It warned that if parents stopped showing love towards the family or each other, the children would grow up without believing in love. Love can only be learned by loving, and can only be taught by a role model. And from love comes faith—faith in family, ourselves, and in life itself.

Hopefully we have set a good role model at home, and you have learned these lessons well. Always remember that love never fears, and that from love comes faith.

Hope you have a wonderful day!

Love,
Mom

■ Not the End of the World

Dear Tim:

It was very cloudy this morning. The grayish sky affected my mood as well, compounded by a newspaper story that a 12-year-old girl just committed suicide. Tears welled up in my eyes as I read the account of how she took her own life.

The story reminded me of your friend Johnny, that golden-haired cute little boy, whom we used to pick up on the way to soccer practice. Then, on an early spring morning, he jumped from a bridge on Route 40 to end his young life of only 13 years.

After the incident, I went many times to your school, concerned about the trauma and confusion felt by you and your other schoolmates. I sat in the back of support group meetings to listen to those who poured their heart out, and to share their innermost thoughts. This experience taught me to understand teenagers much better than before, and I was really impressed with the way your school handled the whole situation.

Your school helped the students deal with the incident primarily by listening. They listened to the anger, sadness, sorrow, and confusion freely expressed by all, without criticism or lecturing. They wisely let the students vent their emotions and feelings without passing judgment. Even blind venting and incoherence were respected. When things began to return to normal, the principal invited a psychologist to come to the school to talk about death and suicide.

"Just think of how precious life is," I remember telling you one day. "You are unique, there is only one of you in the whole wide world. No one else can ever take your place. If you do not like yourself and get along with yourself, who will? You must learn to make peace with yourself." That was how I used the opportunity to express my thoughts to you and your brother.

"How wonderful it is to be young!" I remember saying to you. "You have a boundless future ahead of you. Seize upon every opportunity, and don't ever give up on yourself. Johnny chose to end his short life. Of course we miss him very much. But suicide is a negative response to the difficulties of life. It comes when one turns pessimistic and wants to withdraw from this world. Just remember, there are lots of things in life that are worth celebrating. We all have things in life of which to be proud. We should savor them each day of our lives."

Do you remember the song I taught you and your brother as children? It went like this, "The sun that goes down at dusk will come up again next morning. The flowers that wither on the vine will bloom again next year...."

Yes, go to bed and tomorrow will always be a new day. No matter what happens, it will not be the end of the world. From that time on, "it's not the end of the world" became the most frequently repeated phrase in our home when you were young. You learned to be optimistic and greeted the rising sun with smiles every morning. Although Johnny's suicide brought sadness to the neighborhood, we all learned that life must go on. The overhanging gray clouds slowly dissipated with time.

Every step of life is part of a learning process. In your teenage years, you learned to make friends and have fun, but you also began to learn about life and death. I give my blessing

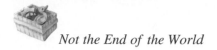

to all young adults out there, and hope that they also understand the importance of that lesson. Sometimes there are bumps and moments of loneliness on the road of life, but they will pass. Life has many faces and many facets. Growing up means learning this truth. Don't ever be afraid that it's the end of the world. Every day is a new day and a new beginning.

Love,
Mom

■ Reap What You Sow

Dear Tim:

Some friends from out of town came to visit today. I took them to see the Dr. Hu Shih Memorial Hall in Academia Sinica. It was, in fact, just a small house, and not very attractive at that.

But what I wanted to show them is the abundant liberal arts spirit symbolized by the building in which he lived. In my student years, Dr. Hu's motto, "plant first what you wish to harvest," left an indelible mark upon me. I have always believed that there is nothing in the world that one can harvest without sweat and tears. Maybe that was the reason I wanted to show them this house.

When you were little, there were always activities at school which required active participation by students. It is quite in vogue now in Taipei, people call it DIY, do it yourself. In your days, we used to enjoy doing these things together. Sometimes it was just one seed or a tiny sprout, at other times a piece of wood or a sheath of colored paper.

We had to plant the seed or the sprout in a pot or in our garden, water it and add fertilizer for it to grow. We also had to figure out what things to make out of the wood or the colored paper. We really threw ourselves into the game, although maybe it shouldn't be called a game, because the learning process itself was so fascinating and more interesting than playing games.

Come to think of it, life itself is a Do-It-Yourself game. You must plant it yourself, and there are no shortcuts. The whole process is uplifting because you do it with all your heart and with your own hands.

When Dr. Hu Shih encouraged others to write Chinese the way it is currently spoken, not how our ancestors spoke it hundreds of years ago, he ran into tremendous roadblocks along the way. But he pointed out that "plant melons and you will harvest melons, plant beans and you will harvest beans." These words from experience are the truth that will stand the test of time.

As a student of design, you know that experience should be the foundation of truth. Without genuinely experiencing something, one cannot gain true knowledge. And without knowledge, one has no motivation to act. This is true in every area of our daily life.

Just think, if someone else controls your decision-making, how can you exert yourself to accomplish anything? If we had forced you to study a subject we chose for you but in which you had no interest at all, why should you burn the midnight oil in order to excel? "Reap what you sow" really is the simplest of truths, but it has so often been neglected in life.

Coming out of Dr. Hu's Memorial Hall, my friend suddenly told me, "I realize now why my son did not do well in his study, because it was I who made all the decisions for him, including his school work and his choice of friends. This is my harvest today."

I wondered whether I should chalk that up as my good deed for the day.

Love,
Mom

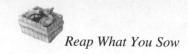
Reap What You Sow

■ Happiness Is Doing What You Enjoy

Dear Tim:

Three senior high school students visited me today. Their teacher asked them to interview an author for their class assignment. They chose me as their subject, and came to talk about writing, as well as why and how I became a writer, or career planning as they call it.

The interview reminded me that many things actually started by accident. When I was young, I may have accidentally written an article that received a teacher's praise, or won a speech competition, or even gained the upper hand in a debate (I used to like to debate). Whatever it was, encouragement and praise always helped me to be confident of myself, teaching me not to be afraid of others.

All these, of course, must originate from personal enjoyment in what one does. If you always do what you enjoy, with praise and encouragement, you will grow up to become proficient in what you do, as I did in writing. On the contrary, with disapproval, mockery or criticism, one would very likely have given up on opportunities to develop and to be creative.

My teachers at elementary and high schools were of tremendous help to me. I believe that every child has lots of dreams of what he or she wants to be when they grow up. Most such dreams vanish with time, while some may be fulfilled over a lifetime. A great deal depends on their teachers' attitudes towards the student.

Do you remember, Tim, when you were in second or third grade and you made a cross-stitch kerchief with "Mommy I love you" on it as a Mother's Day present for me? Your teacher was so amused that you were the only boy in her class who cared to do needlework, that she made it a "big deal" by publicly commending your effort. She produced exactly the opposite effect, because it embarrassed you so much that you dropped out of her crafts class. After the age of eight, you never touched sewing materials again. That was a perfect example of how a teacher's attitude can influence a child's inspiration. Fortunately, your inspiration was not killed. You found other ways to express your creativity and finally ended up in automobile design.

As to career planning, I frankly had no idea of what I would do with my life when I was so young and innocent. There is no way to foresee what the future may bring. All we can do is to have a focus on those things we enjoy, and develop our potential to the fullest. There are endless possibilities in life, and it is not necessary for children to have very specific goals and grandiose plans at an early age. That can be too much pressure for a child to bear.

The mythologist, Joseph Campbell, once said, "A hero's journey is to find the path to himself." I often told you and your brother that you have to find your own niche in life, based on your own talents and on what you do best. If a child studies only for the sake of his parents, or simply aims to be at the top of his class, then that child's life has meaning only in the view of other people. He may turn out to be unhappy later in life, bitterly questioning the meaning of his own success. This is what I want you to understand and be responsible for by yourself.

Love,
Mom

■ Talking to Myself

Dear Tim:

These days I have been kept very busy with workshops and lectures for parent development groups of local schools, so I am a little late getting back to you either by letter or by e-mail.

I learned a lot from these activities. Rather than just giving speeches, I prefer to conduct a dialogue with parents. Two-way conversations made everyone more relaxed, and more effective in sharing ideas and practical tips about raising children. I am sure you remember what I did at your school when you were young.

That was the time of your adolescence. Typically, teenagers during that period like to be seen as cool and carefree, even though deep down inside they may be full of self-doubts and anxieties, which is only normal. Combined with hormonal changes at that age, this makes teenagers very temperamental and rebellious. Often the targets of their aggression are their parents,

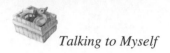

relatives, or close friends. Because of emotional instability, they can be rude or careless with their words, which they often regret afterwards.

To help teenagers to understand this problem and reflect upon their own behavior, I asked each one of them to "talk to yourself," and that included you and your brother. This idea actually evolved from what I heard from these adolescents through in-depth interviews. They frequently told me:

"When I yelled at my parents, deep down inside, I actually hated myself."

"Whenever I lost patience with my siblings, I felt bad about it afterwards."

"I despised myself if I said 'yes' when I should have said 'no.'"

"I felt very sorry when I did not keep a promise to complete a task or chore."

"I always regretted it when I knew I could have offered help, but selfishly refused to do so."

Such guilt and regret can leave lasting impressions, and can negatively affect a teenager's behavior without proper counseling and guidance. Adolescents need opportunities to express these emotions in ways that are not negative. That was why I also asked students to express their positive feelings, and to record what deeds or actions gave them this kind of satisfaction:

"When I completed my duty."

"When I knew I'd done my best."

"When I was honest with people."

"When I helped others."

Even mentally recording and reflecting on our feelings can keep our emotions from getting out of balance. In other words, emotional self-awareness or EQ (Emotional Quotient) produces greater self-control. It is a good idea for all of us, from time to time, to write down the deeds which bring us joy or sadness. For example:

"I felt happy when I helped a disabled or elderly person cross the street," or

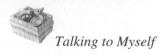

"I regretted it whenever I was rude towards my parents and teachers."

Happiness comes from learning. Every parent always wants their children to grow up well-adjusted, healthy, and happy. Talking with those parents was like revisiting your growing and learning days. I've always believed that everyone is soft at heart, and all children are good and pure. As parents, we should always take the time to learn how to teach and support our children through love and understanding. By doing so without pre-conceived ideas and rash judgment, relationships grow and the family can find happiness together.

Wouldn't you agree?

Love,
Mom

■ Appreciation Accepted

Dear Tim:

I am glad to get your e-mail, saying that you arrived safely back at school at the start of a new academic year. It was nice to have you here over the holidays in your spiritual homeland, after an absence of five years.

I am especially happy that you accompanied me to Chung-Hsing University in Taichung for my presentation to the School of Liberal Arts. It was probably the first time ever that you observed me at "medium range" and listened to me speaking on a stage, while you were sitting in the audience.

What kind of image does a mother have in the eyes of her grown child? I suddenly became curious and wanted to find out. And this was your reply:

"That was my first experience looking at one of my parents from the viewpoint of a grown-up," you wrote. "I felt like a third person sitting there, listening to you speaking about writing, our family, and my own childhood. It really was a wonderful feeling. I was reminded of childhood memories like your reading to me and Dad's taking me fishing. All those times I was learning from you both, but it never felt that way because everything was so much fun. All this was so wonderful, it did not sound like real life."

You went on, "I guess the strongest characteristic in our family is passion—Dad's passion for science, yours clearly for writing, and I am passionate about design. As to my brother, Giles, he is the coolest. He has all, science, writing and thoughts."

Tears welled up in my eyes as I read on, "Mom, thank you for sharing your world of writing with me. Although this vacation in Taiwan was short, it was indeed unforgettable. I felt so fortunate that you insisted I should learn Chinese as a child."

In my mind, I pictured you drinking tea while writing your letter to recall this last visit to Taiwan. I remembered another summer vacation here when you were eight years old. You told me one night, "Mommy, I felt kind of funny on the street today, when I saw so many people who looked like me, with black hair

and dark eyes. I felt my nose tickle as if I were to cry."

I gave you a big hug as I realized that you also inherited my sensitivity — like mother, like son. You were no longer a naughty little boy. You were beginning to observe and reflect on the world for yourself. That was exactly what we were dreaming of, and looked forward to, as parents.

You said in the letter that after this year's visit home, you began to drink Chinese tea. I could not help but applaud the upgrade in your taste, since you used to drink only Coke or ice water. Because of our family and your upbringing, East and West are interchangeable for you, which is to your advantage. Having an understanding and appreciation for both cultures gives you more space to grow and more opportunities in life. There is never any need to choose one above the other, or to look upon either with a narrow point of view.

The boy who was always reluctant to go to Chinese Language School during weekends when he was little now writes me in a serious manner expressing his appreciation! I gladly accept your gratitude, because it demonstrates once again that you will continue to develop full potential of your personality and talents. Keep on going.

Love,
Mom

■ Celebrations

Dear Tim:

It is now graduation season and there are parties everywhere in Taiwan: farewell parties, graduation parties, parties to say thank you to teachers. For families that care about education of their children, and that includes almost everyone in Taiwan, this is indeed the year's most important event.

Whether one is graduating from kindergarten, elementary school, high school, or college, the students celebrating now have accomplished a major step in their lives. Everyone here is aware of this, and excitement and joy are in the air—not only for the graduates, but also for their parents and teachers as well. Even I could sense their joy in these celebrations.

I still remember when you graduated from preschool program. Every child had a small mortar board on their head and held a tiny diploma in their hands. At one point, the whole class dressed as animals—lion, tiger or monkey—and performed an indoor circus show. Parents and teachers were busily taking pictures, and at the same time applauding every performance.

Afterwards, I asked whether you were happy or not, and you responded innocently yet enthusiastically, "I love school. I don't want to graduate!" You were only four and a half years old.

After preschool, you went on to kindergarten, then primary school, junior and senior high. Every day you told me how much you loved to go to school. It was more fun than staying home, you said, because you made new friends and learned new things each day. You learned to overcome your shy nature and became a more independent person. The little hand that refused to let go wanted to move on by itself. The boy who insisted on listening to a story before closing his eyes learned to "show off" by reading the story himself. Each step was a change and growth towards maturity. As parents, your father and I were happy and proud to watch you move step by step towards defining your own identity.

Like every child, you entertained many dreams growing up. You wanted to become a firefighter because you loved fire engines. Then you dreamed of being Batman, Mickey Mouse, a veterinarian, even a garbage truck driver, in that sequence. Your future changed every day and by trying on different personas, you slowly learned about yourself. You also became more aware and concerned about the world around you, which influenced your learning and personal growth.

To make any of our dreams come true, we have to discipline ourselves and turn our dreams first into action, and then into reality. Graduation is the celebration of a completed period of action and learning, a time to review and evaluate our performance, as well as a time to celebrate our efforts and the knowledge gained. Yet every day is a cause to celebrate if we have accomplished our daily work and have done our best. That is something always worthy of applause.

Graduation is a time to look at work that is done, to review and rethink before setting out again. As always, Tim, I am sure you are also looking forward to your own personal goals for learning and growing. For you and to all graduates today, I send my best wishes.

Congratulations!

Love,
Mom

■ Careful with the Internet

Dear Tim:

We are so grateful for high-tech developments, such as those that allow us to communicate with each other via e-mail. Despite the distance between Taiwan and the United States, we can still have heart-to-heart exchanges through the Internet in this shrinking world. Sometimes though, a written letter offers more depth than a phone call or even a face-to-face conversation. At times, verbal communication could fail us, but the written words allow us to convey deeper feelings. This is the reason I still write, because I am used to expressing my thoughts better this way.

You mentioned in your letter that some people use the information highway to have conversations all over the world, make friends and form new relationships. But the danger also exists that one may sit in front of the computer all day, engage in frivolous chatting and, worse still, fall into all kinds of traps. That led you into the question of distrust between people.

Coincidentally, your comment arrived just as I want to start the discussion of Internet friendship among young people here. Since we are never face-to-face on the Internet, it is especially comfortable for shy persons who prefer facing a computer screen to interacting with people directly. This creates opportunities for unscrupulous businessmen to exploit the Internet, using the technology to victimize innocent young adults. Internet crime has become a very important issue in this day and age. With more teenagers at their computers over the summer vacation, I wanted to mention a few guidelines we should all keep in mind:

(1) Never give your home address, phone number, school name, or any other personal information to a stranger on the Internet. Do not correspond regularly or exchange photos with anyone on the Internet without letting your parents know. Consult your parents first regarding rendezvous if you plan face-to-face meetings.

(2) If you encounter any pornographic, violent language or pictures, let your parents know about it immediately. Give your

parents the Internet address of the source or save a print-out, so that they can lodge complaints with the sender or the proper authorities.

(3) In case you run into a sensitive situation, whether it involves privacy, violence or other painful issues, let your parents know. Do not try to deal with these issues alone.

In principle, people should respect and trust each other. But with the explosion of the information age, all sorts of strange things have happened, creating a sad state of affairs that has brewed distrust and created distance between people. There are countless stories which you must have also heard in the United States, such as the middle-aged man who pretended to be a young woman, or the personable friend who turned out to be a salesman making a pitch. To make sense of what you see on the screen—or what may be happening behind the screen—you must learn to use good judgment to discern the real from the fake, the good from the bad.

The dangers of the information superhighway are different from those of the automotive highway. In a car, an accident is

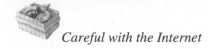

usually the result of careless driving, but on the Internet, it is often an intentional effort by someone to intrude on your privacy and disrupt your peaceful life.

Nonetheless, do not let these dangers prevent you from using the Internet wisely and well. The convenience of new technology gives us easy access to all types of knowledge. People are now exploring Mars, after walking on the moon decades ago. Great discoveries in space and science have enriched our learning opportunities, and enabled us to see more wonders of the universe. You may actually tour the moon or Mars someday. You should certainly use the technology and resources available to educate yourself, so that you will be ready when the opportunity arises.

Love,
Mom

■ Learn to Protect Yourself

Dear Tim:

Recently, I conducted a number of workshops on parenting, and there were many questions raised about how to raise children in a safe environment. Mothers with adolescent daughters, in particular, were very much concerned with such things as sexual harassment, violence, and rape. There have been so many reported cases of such incidents that the joy and innocence of bringing up girls seem to vanish. Parents of teenage girls would say, with a tinge of envy, to those who have only sons, "How nice it is you don't have to worry at all! Boys are safer."

But is it true? Is it wise or justified for parents to treat boys differently than girls? According to a 1990 U.S. Department of Justice report, one in every four girls suffered from some kind of sexual harassment. The same survey revealed that one in every six boys had the same kind of experience. It is apparent that both boys and girls must learn how to deal with difficult situations for their own protection.

I recall that in the United States, grade schools as well as junior high schools teach students on how to protect themselves from harassment. That was valuable information then, and I think it is worth sharing now. Students are taught that if anyone ever approaches them with inappropriate language or behavior, they should react immediately by the following rules:

(1) Start by saying "I don't like what you are doing" with a firm voice and in a straightforward manner. Keep a serious expression, and no smiles. No matter if you are a boy or a girl, the person responsible for such inappropriate behavior will get the message and know that he can't get away with it, now or in the future. When you express your true feelings clearly, you are not only taking the first step towards self-respect, you are also telling the listener that he cannot take advantage of you.

(2) Record the place, date, and time as well as the exact words and/or behavior used. This can be used as evidence later, if necessary. Although you do not need to be oversensitive or rude, you must be firm and clear. This awareness and attitude

should be developed at an early age.

(3) Report the event to your parents, teachers, friends or classmates.

(4) Let the perpetrator know that such behavior will not go without apology or punishment on his/her part. It is not your job to find an excuse for inappropriate behavior of others, but it is your responsibility to be firm and clear. If your response is vague or ambiguous, such harassment may continue.

Protecting the fundamental rights should be cultivated from an early age. It is not only a means to avoid harassment from others, but also a lesson that others should be treated with respect as well. Young children are often mischievous, but sometimes this kind of behavior can cross the line of impropriety.

Last year a six-year-old boy in North Carolina, who liked to tease the girls in his class, was cited by his school for, of all things, sexual harassment. He was probably just a naughty boy who thought that it was fun to pull a girl's braid until she became angry and cried. I remember discussing this particular

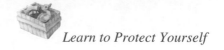

case with you and many older students. The consensus was that there are bound to be students like that in elementary and middle schools. However, this kind of behavior should be addressed as soon as possible, so that it does not continue as students grow older. They must be taught early on, that sexual harassment is never acceptable anywhere, anytime.

From the time you were a small boy, I have tried to teach you self-respect as well as to respect all others. From respect, we learn to care for ourselves and for others. By caring, we help to create peace. I hope that children today learn this, and that your generation will enjoy a life of mutual respect and harmony.

Love,
Mom

Epilogue

Dear Mom:

It is now mid-June and the rainy season has begun here in Japan. The morning commute is full of salarymen in matching black suits hurrying across wet streets to the nearest train station. On the train everyone vies for that last seat against the crush of people and oppressive humidity.

Under these conditions, it is admittedly difficult to keep a smile on one's face. At times, it is even hard to keep your eyes looking up, so heavy is the mass of air and people. Yet I try to remain optimistic and appreciative of the opportunity to be here for awhile and experience this very different culture and lifestyle.

To think back to our last series of letters, when I was in school in California while you and Dad were in Taiwan, I never would have imagined that my career would carry me from the US to Europe, and then to Japan. I am certainly grateful for the opportunities I have been granted and also a little amazed at the turns life has taken.

I guess at any point in time, it is difficult to see where your life may lead, but what I learned from you and Dad is that doing your best at a given moment will always lead you to the next step and the next opportunity. This has proven true even when I didn't know what that next step would be, or where it might take me. Focusing on the task at hand, though, doing my best and giving my all became an objective in and of itself. The process became the goal, and the rest seems to have taken care of itself.

When I take a moment to step outside of the daily rush and reflect—as you have taught me to do—on where I have been and what life has given me, I am happy to realize that I have followed the turns in my life and remain true to my path. As you have quoted from Joseph Campbell, "A hero's journey is to find the path to himself," and that, perhaps, is the most fundamental of all pursuits.

That pursuit has shown me unbelievable places and introduced me to incredible individuals and experiences that have helped me along my way. In so doing, they have taught me to trust the path I am on and to develop a true sense of contentment, something more precious than anything else they could offer.

I am grateful that you and Dad taught me the gift of finding contentment in life, by encouraging me to follow life's surprises and to pursue a path that is meaningful to me. With that in mind, I am able to smile a little to myself, oblivious to the crowds of commuters that surround me on the morning train, unaffected by the rain that continues to fall outside.

Much love from Japan,
Tim
June 12, 2004

(A Letter from Dr. Jane Vella to Jane Wan)

Dear Jane,

I smile when you call me "your teacher" and recall the day we met in 1978 at North Carolina State University. You were such an earnest young mother, eager to start a career as a graduate student in library science. When I heard your story and read your sparkling eyes as you described your writing, I took a bold step. "Jane," I said, "You are destined to write the books, not to catalogue them!"

You joined me as a full partner in my first year of teaching at the university, along with Michael Chalmers from England. The southern woman who was the department secretary used to say she could not understand any one of us—we all talked funny!

We did good research in the field, inviting stories from adults who had just learned to read after years of being "in the closet" as illiterates. Your own studies culminated in a wonderful day with a committee of professors and me, as you did your Master's defense. They were utterly charmed, as I have always been.

The boys grew up, Jason's career thrived as he brought North Carolina State University to China and back again! I created JUBILEE Center and went round the world teaching.

We created The China Center together, here in Raleigh,

hoping to teach southern folks the glory of the East. You went from professional glory to glory with book after book, article after article. We spoke constantly of writing together. Finally, an opportunity arose as you spoke of interest in publishing *Letters to My Son* in English and in Chinese. So we collaborate at last to move your Chinese prose into English.

The first thing I will do in heaven is to ask to read your works in Chinese! I know that our rendition of your writing, even of this simple book, fails to capture the beauty of the Chinese phrase, the rhythm and melody, the nuances of metaphor that exist in Chinese.

However, it is a collaboration I am proud of. And it proves what I have known all along—you are *my* teacher! And my friend.

Thank you!

Jane

生字表
Vocabulary

p. 72～75

overshadow [ˌovɚˈʃædo] *v.* 使相形見絀，勝過

upbeat [ˈʌpˌbit] *adj.* 開朗的，樂觀的

tantrum [ˈtæntrəm] *n.* 發脾氣

tongue-in-cheek 　諷刺的

p. 76～79

resourceful [rɪˈsorsfəl] *adj.* 善於隨機應變的，足智多謀的

adept [əˈdɛpt] *adj.* 熟練的，精通的

worn out 　破舊的，不能再用的

recollection [ˌrɛkəˈlɛkʃən] *n.* 回憶，記憶

p. 80～83

nostalgia [nɑˈstældʒɪə] *n.* 懷舊之情

tug-of-war 　拔河

frugal [ˈfrʊgl] *adj.* 節儉的

permeate [ˈpɝmɪˌet] *v.* 瀰漫，充滿

p. 84～87

grandeur [ˈgrændʒɚ] *n.* 雄偉，壯觀

eventuality [ɪˌvɛntʃuˈælətɪ] *n.* 可能發生的事情

opt [ɑpt] *v.* 選擇

p. 92～95

periodical [ˌpɪrɪˈɑdɪkl̩] *n.* 期刊，雜誌
toddler [ˈtɑdlə] *n.* 初學步的幼兒

p. 96～99

connotation [ˌkɑnəˈteʃən] *n.* 言外之意
exuberant [ɪgˈzjubərənt] *adj.* 充滿活力的，精力旺盛的
death sentence　　死刑

p. 100～103

hide-and-seek　　捉迷藏
commendation [ˌkɑmənˈdeʃən] *n.* 獎狀
memorabilia [ˌmɛmərəˈbɪlɪə] *n.* 值得紀念的事物
imbue [ɪmˈbju] *v.* 灌輸（思想、感情等）

p. 104～107

abjection [æbˈdʒɛkʃən] *n.* 落魄
enviable [ˈɛnvɪəbl̩] *adj.* 值得羨慕的

p. 108～112

dampen [ˈdæmpən] *v.* 使意志消沈
taboo [təˈbu] *n.* 禁忌
pronounced [prəˈnaʊnst] *adj.* 明顯的
saggy [ˈsægɪ] *adj.* 鬆垮的

p. 113～116

blurt [blɜt] *v.* 不經意說出，脫口而出

bite off more than one can chew　承擔力所不及之事

p. 117～119

erode [ɪˋrod] *v.* 腐蝕

p. 120～123

vent [vɛnt] *v.* （情緒的）宣洩

incoherence [ˌɪnkoˋhɪrəns] *n.* 沒有條理

savor [ˋsevɚ] *v.* 品味

dissipate [ˋdɪsəˌpet] *v.* 驅散，使消散

facet [ˋfæsɪt] *n.* （事情、問題的）一個方面

p. 124～126

indelible [ɪnˋdɛləbḷ] *adj.* 難以去除的

shortcut [ˋʃɔrtˌkʌt] *n.* 捷徑

p. 128～131

proficient [prəˋfɪʃənt] *adj.* 精通的，熟練的

commend [kəˋmɛnd] *v.* 讚揚

niche [nɪtʃ] *n.* 適當的位置

p. 132～135

two-way conversation　雙向溝通

counsel [`kaʊnsl̩] *n.* 建議，忠告

p. 137～140

interchangeable [ˌɪntɚˋtʃendʒəbl̩] *adj.* 可互換的，可取代的

p. 141～143

mortar board　（畢業典禮時戴的）方頂帽

sequence [`sikwəns] *n.* 順序，次序

p. 144～147

rendezvous [`rɑndəˏvu] *n.* 會面，約會

pornographic [ˌpɔrnəˋgræfɪk] *adj.* 色情的

discern [dɪˋzɝn] *v.* 辨別

disrupt [dɪsˋrʌpt] *v.* 使混亂

p. 148～151

harassment [həˋræsmənt] *v.* 騷擾

rape [rep] *v.* 強暴

perpetrator [`pɝpəˏtretɚ] *n.* 作惡者，犯罪者

impropriety [ˌɪmprəˋpraɪətɪ] *n.* 不適當

譯者 石 廷

　　自北卡州立大學建築系畢業後，再進入加州帕沙第納藝術中心設計學院交通運輸工具設計系。從那時候起，他就在美國、歐洲及亞洲擔任汽車設計師。他的興趣包括藝術欣賞、跳舞和滑雪，當然，還有汽車。

After graduating from North Carolina State University with a degree in Architecture, Tim Shih went on to study Transportation Design at Art Center College of Design in California. Since then, he has been working as a car designer in the US, Europe, and Asia. His hobbies include art, dance, snowboarding, and—of course—cars.

譯者 Dr. Jane Vella

　　簡維理博士 (Dr. Jane Vella) 與簡宛女士已有 25 年的深厚友誼及合作關係。維理博士在成人學習教育方面的著作豐富，她的著作《Learning to Listen, Learning to Teach》在全世界多所大專院校被廣泛選用。維理博士畢業於美國麻州大學安默斯特分校，紐約佛漢大學，及紐約市立大學亨特學院，她的工作足跡遍及世界超過 40 個國家，現退休定居於美國北卡羅來納州首府洛麗市，繼續從事成人學習教育研究。

　　Jane Vella has written extensively on adult learning. Her book *Learning to Listen, Learning to Teach* (Jossey Bass/Wiley 2002) is used in universities and colleges throughout the world. Dr. Vella studied at the University of Massachusetts at Amherst, Fordham University in New York and Hunter College in New York City. She has worked in more than forty countries worldwide. She is presently retired in Raleigh, North Carolina, continuing her research on adult learning. She celebrates her twenty-five years of collaboration and friendship with Jane Wan.